THE SILVER SPURS HOME FOR AGING COWGIRLS

The Silver Spurs Series: Book One

by

Laura Hesse

Running L Productions   Vancouver Island, B.C.

The Silver Spurs Home for Aging Cowgirls/by Laura Hesse

ISBN (print book): 978-1999077419

Cover Design by: AutumnSky, Selfpubbookcovers.com

Distributed Worldwide on Amazon

Publisher: Running L Productions, Vancouver Island, British Columbia Canada.

Publisher Website: www.runninglproductions.com

Dedication

To the wonderful horses and dogs in my life,
may we meet again. To all the amazing horsemen and
horsewomen out there, thanks for sharing your knowledge and
boundless energy. To the ranchers and their families who work
tirelessly and selflessly to feed the multitudes and maintain their
way of life, God bless.
And...

To the men and women in the military who give their all to keep
us safe from harm, a heartfelt 'thank you'.

Acknowledgements

This story was a wild and crazy ride to write. It had been gelling in my mind for several years before I sat down and put pen to paper. While there is no swearing, there is some questionable behaviour by our four saucy seniors which might not be to everyone's tastes; but, hey it is a naughty western adult comedy.

A huge thank you to my friend, Dee Gallant, the 'Cougar Whisperer' from Vancouver Island. It is also thanks to Dee that I currently have a wonderful rescue dog in my life.

The Saint Bernard in the story is a real dog as is the paint stallion named 'Add a Patch'. Bulldozer and Patch were wonderful buddies who shared in my life's adventures. May we meet again.

A special thank you goes out to my friends, Deb and Cheryl, for being my sounding board.

Contents

THE SILVER SPURS HOME FOR AGING COWGIRLS

The Silver Spurs Series: Book One

Prelude – five years earlier

A man on a horse is spiritually as well as physically bigger than a man on foot.
John Steinbeck

An army green jeep drove up the long winding lane that lead to the sprawling Montana family ranch, dust billowing out behind it. A hundred red and white Herefords and five ranch horses grazed along the split railed log fence that bordered the drive. One horse, a big sorrel with four white stockings and a lightning blaze down the center of its face, watched the vehicle's progress with interest. The rest of the herd continued to graze with indifference.

The sun beat down on the browning pastures beyond the fence line. Blue-green mountains hovered over the ranch, appearing to hang from the sky like patio lanterns in the heat haze of the afternoon.

Inside the old barn, its sides faded by years of blistering hot sun, a white-haired old man with a sweat stained grey Stetson, drooping white moustache, and piercing hazel eyes, stopped in mid-sweep as the Jeep pulled up in front of the faded two-storey gabled ranch house that had been in the Montana family for three generations.

A black and white Border collie, its muzzle white with age, lay in a spot by the sun, warming its fragile bones on the hot concrete.

Sam Montana's hands trembled slightly as he saw the two immaculately uniformed Marines exit the Jeep, a tall gangly lieutenant and a short, broad shouldered sergeant. The sergeant reached inside the Jeep and reverently took out a folded flag.

Sam propped the straw broom against the wall, wiped the sweat from his brow with a crumpled handkerchief that he pulled from his jeans pocket, and then squared his shoulders before walking purposefully across the dirt yard towards the house, the Border collie trotting along after him.

A handsome youthful woman with flushed cheeks, peach coloured hair, and sky-blue eyes pushed open the screen door and stepped out onto the porch. She balanced a three-year-old little girl, the image of her mother, on one hip. The little girl flipped over one of her mother's silver conch earrings and giggled with delight. Emma Montana, newly widowed, absently pulled the earrings out of her daughter's grasp.

Behind Emma followed an adolescent boy with black hair, hazel eyes, and a calm quietness about him that made him seem much older than his eight years. His eyes bore a striking resemblance to the old man's.

"Sorry for your loss, ma'am," the lieutenant said.

The woman nodded, her red-rimmed eyes closing as she fought to compose herself. Words of acknowledgement were left unspoken lest the grief that had her in a stranglehold burst forth. She didn't want to cry in front of her children, especially her daughter who didn't understand that daddy wasn't coming home again.

Sam climbed the two steps onto the porch and took the wriggling three-year-old from her mother's arms. He gently kissed the toddler on the top of the head.

"Grandpa," the little girl chirped, beaming up at her grandfather.

"Jenny-penny," he returned, his voice weakened by grief.

"Grandpa, a-okay," his granddaughter asked, her brow knit with worry. Jenny was a bright child and though not understanding what was going on, she sensed the sadness in her family.

"Grandpa's heart aches," Sam replied, pointing to his heart.

Jenny hugged him close and planted a loud kiss on his cheek.

"Jenny make it better," the girl gushed. "Jocko make it better too."

The old man smiled as he hugged his granddaughter back. The Border collie yawned and wagged its tail, its rheumy eyes fixed lovingly on the girl.

"I'm sorry we couldn't bring him home," the sergeant added, handing Emma the folded flag. He was broad shouldered and solid of frame with a wide jaw, bronzed skin, and eyes and hair the color of polished black walnut.

4

Emma reached for the flag, but her hands shook so hard that she couldn't hold it.

Her son stepped forward and took the flag from the marine and then handed it to his mother, slowly closing his hands around hers to stop them from shaking.

Tears welled in Emma's eyes as she held the flag against her breast. Suddenly her face reddened, and she spun on her heel. She raced into the house; the porch screen door slamming shut behind her.

The marines took no offence. They took two steps backwards and then snapped a salute to the boy.

BJ Montana snapped a smart salute right back.

The lieutenant grinned, and did an about face, returning to the Jeep, his duty done.

"I promised Cleve that if anything ever happened to him, I would be there for you," Sergeant Gus Rodriquez explained, his words falling flat.

"Thank you, sir," BJ replied crisply, "but it's my job to look after my mum now."

"It's good of you to come all this way, Gus," Sam thanked the young marine. "I know Emma appreciated it, even if she couldn't say it."

"Your son was my best friend, Mr Montana. I had to come," Gus stuttered.

An awkward stillness fell between the two men and the boy standing protectively on the front porch, each of them battling to hold back the tidal wave of grief that enveloped their hearts. Jenny looked from one to the other of them.

"I understand from the Base Commander's phone call that you're shipping out again," Sam asked, ending the gulf of silence.

"Yes, sir," Gus agreed.

"Then God be with you, son," Sam said, lowering his granddaughter to the ground. He extended a hand and the two men shook, grips strong and firm.

Jenny batted her eyes at the handsome marine, one finger twirling in the curls of red hair that framed her pretty face.

"Looks like you have a fan," Sam chortled.

Gus smiled and knelt in front of Jenny.

"I hope I see you again one day," Gus beamed.

Jenny flew into his arms.

Gus wrapped his arms around his best friend's daughter and hugged her close. He laughed aloud. The Border collie joined in the hug, tail wagging, not wanting to be left out. The old dog licked the marine's face.

"You're always welcome here," Sam warbled, his baritone voice cracking with emotion.

"Thank you, sir," Gus replied hoarsely, standing up.

The men shook hands one more time before Gus strode back to the Jeep. He saw Emma watching him through the front bay window. She still clasped the flag to her breast. He sighed heavily and waved goodbye. She lifted a limp hand in return.

Chapter One – present day

There are no women or horses without shortcomings.
French Proverb

Sam sat on the front porch in his favourite rocking chair. He had made it for his wife and sitting in it made the world a better place. Memories of his beautiful Adelaide rocking their newborn son to sleep while she sipped a cup of mint tea made him smile. The memories were bittersweet but wasn't the past always that way. In truth, he was at the age when the images he held crisp in his mind were more comfort than looking at an album full of fading photographs.

As he chewed on the end of his unlit pipe, he was grateful for what the good Lord had left him: a charming and devoted daughter-in-law and two priceless grandchildren. In his heart, though, he knew things weren't picture perfect.

He had sold the last of the cattle last spring in order to pay the ranch's exorbitant land taxes. The price of real estate in the valley had skyrocketed in the past few years. It had already forced some of his lifelong friends and neighbours to sell out.

He and Emma had brainstormed last year, first trying a Bed & Bale, a unique concept where folks with horses came to stay and take advantage of the ranch's proximity to the mountains, but the Diamond Bar, two ranches over, had been doing it for years and he and Emma hadn't been able to compete. They had thought of starting up dude rides too, but once again the Diamond Bar already had that market cornered.

Sometimes, he wondered if he was hanging on to a lifestyle that was a thing of the past or if the Devil was whispering in his ear urging him to go past the point of no return.

He looked longingly at the mountain range beyond the ranch's borders, wishing he was moving a herd up into the cooler summer pastures instead of sitting on the porch in a rocking chair dreaming about it.

His precocious granddaughter was fighting a losing battle in the front yard with the little red roan appaloosa pony that he had bought for a song at a meat auction last year.

"Grandpa, Rosie won't listen to me," Jenny cried, blowing a stray piece of her curly red hair out of her face.

Sam chuckled. The pony and his eight-year-old granddaughter were a sight, both sporting a riotous array of red freckles, the first on its rump, the second on her face.

"Exactly what are you trying to accomplish, Jenny-penny," he asked, watching them go around and around in ever tighter circles.

"She's trying to get Rosie to spin on her haunches," BJ replied, his big buckskin ranch horse looking as much amused as its rider.

"Ahhh," Sam nodded in understanding.

"Did you practice the groundwork I taught you in the ring before you got on her," BJ asked, already knowing the answer.

"Of course not," she seethed, her eyes flashing with anger. "What good is groundwork if you can't do what you do ad nauseam in the saddle?"

Sam burst out laughing, realizing that reality was sometimes better than a dream. In truth, he had everything any man could ever wish for right in front of him.

"Ad nauseam is it," he chortled.

Jenny loved picking up new words and using them… ad nauseam.

"You keep going around and around like that and you're going to barf," BJ quipped. "Either that or you're gonna make that pony fall over."

"Rosie does look a bit dizzy," Sam chortled.

Jenny reined in her pony. She glowered at her brother. The pony looked as disgruntled as its rider, with its tail hanging low beneath its legs and its ears pinned back in annoyance. The tiny appaloosa lifted its tail and farted.

Emma laughed merrily as she pushed the door open and wandered out on the porch, a flour speckled apron wrapped around her waist. She tucked her long faux leather skirt around her legs and then sat down in a chair beside her father-in-law, beaded earrings and Navaho belt rustling as she did so.

"What's going on," she asked innocently.

"Apparently, groundwork to improve your horse's training is nauseous," Sam declared, pointing towards his granddaughter with the pipe.

"Then perhaps homework and chores will fix that," Emma offered. "There's a sink full of dirty dishes and fingerprints all over the bathroom mirror that need washing. Oh, yes, and the table needs setting for dinner."

"Don't forget the living room, there's at least a foot of dust on the coffee table," Sam agreed.

"Undeniably," Emma added, using another one of Jenny's latest favourites.

"Moommmm. Grandddpaaaa," Jenny pleaded. "I can't put Rosie away now, not when she wouldn't do what I wanted her to do. What kind of example would I be setting?"

Emma and Sam smothered a chuckle.

"She's got you there," BJ chirped. "It would be bad horsemanship."

"Haven't you got a barn to clean," the old cowboy scolded his grandson.

"After dinner, he does," Emma said. "Put those horses away and come in and clean up."

"Yes, ma'am," BJ replied, whirling his Quarter horse around on its haunches and trotting away. He grinned over his shoulder at his sister.

"He's such a show-off," Jenny whispered to her pony.

Emma watched her children ride off, the laughter dying on her lips.

"While the kids aren't within ear shot, we've got some serious things to talk about, Sam."

"Yeah, I've been thinking on it too," he sighed wearily.

Sam lit his pipe. A blue plume of tobacco drifted away on the breeze.

"We're at the end of it. There's only seven hundred dollars left in the savings account and next month's mortgage payment and interest on our credit cards will take care of that," Emma continued. "My widow's allowance and your Old Age Security aren't covering our monthly expenses anymore. I have no idea how we're going to pay the land taxes this year."

"Well, we got no more cows," Sam said thoughtfully. "We could sell three of the horses. Boomer won't fetch more than meat prices, though. He's just too old. Penny and Checkers are worth a bit though. They still got game."

"You can't sell Boomer. He's family and Checkers is your cutting horse. I hate to lose Penny, but if I want to go riding, I can always borrow Bucky from BJ."

"Don't need a cutting horse when you ain't got no cows to cut," Sam said matter-of-factly.

"That still won't get us out of the debt we're in. And what about the house," she cried, "the roof needs repairing before winter and the stove is close to giving up the ghost. That doesn't even include that old oil furnace, which is costing us a fortune to run. This place is just too darn big to maintain."

"The roof'll hold another season and this old house'll be standing long after I'm gone and you too for that matter," he replied stiffly. "Be grateful for it."

"I am, Sam, just overwhelmed by all the red ink. I was thinking that it's time I got a job. I heard that the Grocery Mart is hiring."

"You got a job… raising those kids," he growled.

In the distance, they saw the sheriff's big Suburban pulling a short box horse trailer turn off the highway and into their driveway.

"Fancy that, company's coming right in time for dinner," Sam drawled, ending the conversation.

"We still haven't finished talking."

"I know," Sam acknowledged.

"What do you think is in the trailer?"

"We'll find out soon enough."

BJ and Jenny raced around the corner, arms pumping. BJ slowed slightly so that Jenny could beat him.

"Hah, beat you again," Jenny cried breathlessly.

"Yep, you sure did." BJ grinned.

"What do think the sheriff is hauling," Jenny asked her grandfather.

Sam shrugged as he stood up. He placed his pipe in the clay holder that Jenny had made him last Christmas. It was supposed to be a frog but looked more like a lump of green manure than a reptile.

Sam sauntered down the steps and across the yard as the beige Suburban circled the lane and pulled up in front of the house.

"Hey, Sheriff, what ya got in the trailer," Jenny yelled, bouncing along after her grandfather.

"Why don't you let the sheriff get out of the car first," Emma chastised her daughter, joining her daughter- and father-in-law in the middle of the sun-baked laneway.

"Do I have to," Jenny blushed.

"Yes, you do. Mind your manners," Emma ordered the little girl.

"Must be pretty short whatever it is. That's an awfully small trailer," BJ motioned towards the tiny wooden sided trailer.

"How y'all doing today," Sheriff Cole Trane asked as he stepped out of the SUV.

"Good timing, young feller," Sam joked, tipping his hat back on his head. Everyone in the valley knew that the sheriff was sweet on his daughter-in-law, including Emma.

Thirty-five-year-old Sheriff Cole Trane was handsome in a boy next door kind of way. He had short cropped brown hair, apple dumpling cheeks, brown eyes, an open earnest face, and a crooked nose because drunks seemed to always want to punch him in it. He was the youngest sheriff ever elected in the county.

"Well, I'm hoping you folks can open your heart and stable until I can find this poor soul a permanent home," Cole said.

"What is it," Jenny asked, jumping up and down to see over top of the rear tail gate. "Let me see, let me see."

"Well, before you say 'yeah' or 'nay', let me tell you a bit about him. I've traced some of his history to a rescue lady back East, and then to some prospector down south, but I suspect he started in California with one of the wild herds there."

"There're no wild horses in California," Emma replied, puzzled.

"Well, ya see, that there is where it gets complicated," Cole answered, suddenly finding his worn cowboy boots of immense interest.

"This can't be good," Sam drawled.

BJ walked around and stood on the rear bumper of the trailer. He leaned forward and peeked inside the trailer. He started to giggle. The giggle turned into a gut busting belly laugh.

"What? What is it," his sister begged him?

The traveller inside the small trailer brayed, a great honking 'heehaw'. The horses in the field snorted in fear and galloped off a few paces and then stopped in one fluid motion to face the frightening sound.

"It's a donkey," Emma yelped, placing a hand over her mouth.

"You've got to be kidding," Sam said, tipping his hat forward and glowering at Cole.

"Well, not just any donkey," replied Cole.

"No," Sam stated adamantly.

"No," Emma echoed her father-in-law.

"Wait, wait, wait! The State will pay for his board," Cole continued.

"Can I see him? Can I? Can I? What's his name," Jenny asked, vibrating in place.

"His name is Mike. He was stolen from the donkey rescue and... excuse the pun... but got used as a drug mule. He was beat on something fierce and they mutilated the poor thing. Mike's a dear old guy, and he didn't deserve what was done to him. The vet pulled the drugs out of him and stitched him up, but he said the trip back to the rescue in Tennessee would be too hard on him. Old Mike's at least fifty, the vet says. What he needs right now is some TLC, and I couldn't think of nicer folks than you to look after him."

"Buttering us up good, are you," Sam muttered.

"Yes, sir, I am, but it's Mike that I'm thinking of," Cole said.

"I bet it is," Sam quipped.

"How much," Emma asked.

"How much what," Cole queried sweetly.

"Cole Trane, I've known you a long time. Don't be smart with me," Emma said. "It isn't that my heart wouldn't fall in love with him… and don't you dare undo that tail gate, BJ… it's just that we can't afford another mouth to feed right now."

Emma blushed.

"I'm sorry, Cole, I don't mean to air our family's troubles, but we just can't afford it, especially an old donkey with vet bills," Emma continued.

"Well, we can pay you a hundred dollars a month for his upkeep and all of his vet bills, if necessary, until the trial date and until the State decides what to do with him," Cole replied, his own cheeks reddening.

Emma looked her father-in-law square in the eye. He held her gaze.

"Don't look at me like that," Sam chortled. "I'm leaving this decision up to you."

"Oh, Mom, we've got to help him," Jenny pleaded. "Pleaaassseee."

The donkey let out another long bray that sounded like a broken foghorn.

BJ stood with his hand on the trailer's tail gate clasp waiting for his mother's nod of approval.

"It can't hurt to take a look at him," BJ cajoled his mother.

"And you wouldn't let us get a new puppy," Jenny pouted.

"All right open it up," Emma conceded, "and we'll make our decision then. And, you two kids, the juries still out so don't get your hopes up."

BJ opened the back of the trailer. He walked inside and returned with the saddest little fellow that the family had ever seen.

The donkey was bone thin and sway backed. One of his ears had been lopped off with what must have been a machete. His muzzle was grey with age and his eyes were a soulful brown. His stomach had a six-inch incision in it, the stitches still fresh from where the vet had removed the drug sachets from his belly.

"Well, ain't that the homeliest critter you've ever seen," Sam muttered.

"He is that," Emma agreed.

"But he's cute," Jenny said, throwing an arm around the donkey's neck.

The donkey named Mike nuzzled the little girl, snuffling her jean pockets, looking for a treat.

Sam chuckled and then walked over to the donkey and ran a gentle hand over the donkey's ribs.

"He sure needs some groceries," Sam concurred.

"Can we keep him mum," BJ asked. "I don't mind looking after the old guy and the sheriff did say that he'd buy his feed."

"I will too," Jenny agreed, looking as baleful as the donkey.

"I'm sure I'll regret this, but okay," Emma agreed.

"Whoopee. Come on, Mikey, you're gonna love it here," Jenny crooned to the one eared old fellow.

BJ grinned as he led the donkey towards the barn, Jenny skipping along beside them, chattering away to the donkey. The donkey didn't seem to mind a bit.

"Come on, Sheriff, you may as well stay for dinner," Sam said with a shake of his head. Maybe he and Emma should have said 'yes' to a new puppy. He wondered what on earth had they gotten themselves into.

"Well, if it isn't too much trouble," Cole said, hat in hand.

"It isn't," Emma replied with a grin.

"Who came up with the name," Sam blurted out, tipping his hat back once again.

"Dee Gallant," Cole blushed.

They heard Mike bray loudly as the kids led him into the barn. In the pasture, the horses stampeded, galloping off across the pasture like a tornado was on their tail.

The Montana family plus one sat at the kitchen table, an old cross beam affair made of cedar, that looked more like a rough-hewn picnic table than a kitchen table, but it had been in the family for years and all the family's names were carved into it including Cleve and Emma's inside a cupid's heart.

Cole piled his plate with cold sliced ham, baked beans, two corn cobs, and a giant wedge of corn bread.

Sam winked at his daughter. She smiled back, pleased.

"So, you said Mike came from Tennessee," Jenny mumbled through a mouth full of corn.

"Manners, Jenny-penny," her grandfather scolded.

"Far as I can tell, old Mike has travelled the country. He used to have a brand in the ear that was cut off. The smugglers didn't figure on him being micro-chipped though. That's how we knew where he came from," Cole answered, digging into the baked beans.

Sam wondered when Cole had last eaten; it looked like the sheriff hadn't had a home-cooked meal in days. Either that or he was trying to impress Emma.

"I guess those rescue folks had his tattoo on record," Sam added.

"Yes, sir," Cole agreed. "It wasn't hard to trace his ownership after that. I believe he was part of a wild herd that got rounded up and auctioned off years ago in California but can't be altogether sure about that. They didn't much care what happened to the donkeys at that time."

"Poor thing has been through the grind, hasn't he," Emma stated.

18

Cole continued to eat, his brow furrowing as if he was thinking long and hard.

Sam and Emma exchanged a quick grin.

Everyone ate in silence for a while, even Jenny who also seemed lost in thought. Sam worried about that. It wasn't always a good thing.

"You know my aunt just opened her house up to a bunch of old folks," Cole remarked casually, reaching for seconds. "It ain't quite a rest home, but more than a boarding house. She's got two widows and a widower living with her. They couldn't live alone anymore and didn't want to be forced into a state-run facility. Aunt Betsy was about to lose her house, like everyone these days. Cost of living just keeps going up and Aunt Betsy lost her job when the manufacturing plant just couldn't compete with the cheap imports. She makes better money now than she did before, let me tell you."

"What kind of money," Emma asked, raising an eyebrow.

Sam glanced sideways at her, none too happy about the turn in conversation.

"She gets three thousand a month per resident, she told me," Cole said. "That includes room and board, looking after their basic needs, and driving them to and from doctor appointments, shopping, and things like that. One of them told me they wanted a hundred and ninety-five dollars per day at a private facility and he thought Aunt Betsy was way undercharging."

"You're kidding me," Emma marvelled, her mouth falling open.

"You're catching flies," Sam grumbled.

Emma's mouth clicked shut. She glared across the table at him.

Good grief, Sam thought, here it comes. She wanted to do it. He could see it in the set of her jaw and the narrowing of her eyes.

"I think it'd be cool," Jenny jumped in.

"No one asked you, young lady," Sam growled.

"Well, it would," she challenged her grandfather.

"Maybe we can find someone like us, you know, who likes horses. What about an old horse trainer who doesn't want to be parted from his horses, but can't look after them anymore? We got lots of room in the barn," BJ suggested.

"That's a brilliant idea, BJ," Emma gasped.

"I think we should take in all cowgirls. I could have a whole houseful of cowgirl grandmas."

Sam choked on a piece of ham.

Emma whacked him on the back.

Sam spat the chunk of ham out onto a napkin.

"I don't need a bunch of old hens telling me what to do in my own home," Sam growled. "I can hear it now: I don't drink coffee, I want tea, don't wash my whites with my colours, don't you smoke your pipe in this house."

"You don't smoke in the house anyway," Emma smirked, laughter making her blue eyes sparkle, "and when have you ever done your own laundry?"

"One day I might," Sam concluded.

"Just saying, its food for thought," Cole noted before digging into a second helping of ham and corn.

Sam glowered.

He glanced across the table at Emma. Her face was almost serene. A gentle smile played thoughtfully across her lips.

Sam hadn't seen a smile like that in a long time.

There was nothing worse than a woman whose wheels were turning. Sam already knew his daughter-in-law was doing the numbers and his opinion on the matter wouldn't mean doodles.

Chapter Two

*A woman needs two animals – the horse of her dreams
and a jackass to pay for it.*

"I think it's a brilliant idea," Emma advised her father-in-law over coffee the next day. "We have four empty rooms upstairs, given that you and BJ moved downstairs during Checkers' foaling and never bothered to move back."

"You want to take in four strangers," Sam said, wagging a finger at her, "all of them with their own way of doing things and their own ideas on how things should go. That is a recipe for disaster."

"And its twelve thousand dollars a month, plus board for their horses if we consider taking in seniors with horses like BJ suggested."

"I don't mind the extra chores if it will help," BJ piped in as he entered the kitchen. "And I can make us a website in no time."

"I don't like it," Sam finished.

"Come on, Grandpa, maybe one of the cowgirl grandmas will be cute and you'll fall in love," Jenny

22

shouted, bouncing down the back stairway into the kitchen on her bottom. Thump, thump, thump, she went until she landed on the kitchen floor.

Sam fixed his granddaughter with an evil look.

Jenny giggled.

Emma grinned.

"You had a grandmother," he grunted.

"Yeah, but I never met her," Jenny countered, "so it doesn't count, and mum's parents died before I was born."

"Don't be rude to your grandfather, Jenny," Emma scolded her daughter.

"Sorry," Jenny mumbled, suitably contrite. "It's true though."

"We wouldn't have to do it forever," Emma pleaded. "By my estimation, five years would do it."

"I'll be ready to go to college by then, so that's fair," BJ added, pouring a glass of milk.

"Is that so," Sam queried the boy.

"It is," BJ returned.

"When did you get so wise," Sam asked him.

"Born that way, I guess."

"It runs in the family," Emma joked.

Sam snorted in amusement.

"I guess it wouldn't hurt to put up one of those website things and see if anyone responds," he grumbled.

"Woo hoo," Jenny yelled, hugging her grandfather.

"We'll be selective, Sam," Emma agreed. "I'll ask for tax returns and references plus first and last month as a deposit."

Sam brooded over his coffee cup.

"I'm gonna go feed Mike," Jenny sang. "I bet the cowgirl grandmas will love him too. Maybe I'll even write a song about him."

"So that old fella warrants a song, but your ole grandpa doesn't," kidded Sam.

Jenny pursed her lips together and thought hard for a moment.

"I can write you one too, but I'm gonna write a song about Mike first," she said.

Sam chuckled despite his forebodings.

"What do we want to call it," BJ asked. "We have to have a business name."

"How about *The Cowgirl's Last Stop,*" Sam chortled.

"People aren't going to die here are they," Jenny wailed.

"Nobody is going to die here, honey," Emma replied.

"Except me," Sam stammered, his voice barely above a whisper.

"Maybe *The Shady Rest Retirement Home* or *The Retirement Home for Equestrians,*" Emma chimed, throwing out some ideas.

"Boring," Jenny said, cheering up.

"*Montana's Retirement Ranch,*" BJ offered.

"Sounds like someplace to drop off unwanted horses," Sam grunted. "We'd be digging holes all over the pasture."

"Yep, we'd have to buy a new backhoe," BJ added.

"We'd run out of space in no time flat," Sam agreed.

"Stop it, you two," Emma fumed.

Sam grunted in response, still miffed about the whole idea.

"How about *The Silver Spurs Retirement Home*," BJ suggested.

"Hmmm, that's catchy," Emma agreed.

"No, it should be *The Silver Spurs Home for Aging Cowgirls*," Jenny shouted gleefully. "Seriously, I want some cowgirl grandmas."

"What happens if your cowgirl grandmas don't like kids," BJ ribbed his sister.

Jenny raised her fists to strike her brother, but her mother caught them in mid-air.

"*The Silver Spurs Home for Aging Cowgirls*," Sam retorted, giving in. "I can live with that."

"I love it," Emma cried happily. "All in favour of calling our new business, *The Silver Spurs Home for Aging Cowgirls*, raise their hands?"

Three sets of hands went up around the table.

Emma and BJ looked earnestly towards Sam. Jenny's glare made it apparent that all the demons in Hell would be released if he didn't comply.

Sam sighed in surrender and lifted his hand.

His granddaughter jumped into his lap and kissed him on the cheek.

"I love you, Grandpa," the pretty girl cooed.

"I love you too, Jenny-penny," he said to his granddaughter, wishing there was another way. At seventy-five, he wasn't about to go back on the rodeo circuit, and he definitely didn't want his daughter-in-law driving fifty miles to town and back every day to work at a job he knew that she would hate. His son, God rest his soul, would turn in his grave at the thought; at least, if he had one, he would. His wife, he knew, was already whirling over and over like a Ferris wheel.

"There, not there," Emma directed as Sam stood on one ladder and BJ on the other, fastening a wood sign over the entry to the ranch.

The sign read: *The Silver Spurs Home for Aging Cowgirls*, the letters chiselled out of the cedar wood in old style western lettering. It had taken Sam four days working with a hammer and chisel to do it. He could have done it in half that time, but he wanted to stay out of Emma's way as she bustled from room to room, painting and cleaning.

The weathered wood sign for the Montana Family Ranch lay in the back of Sam's pickup truck.

"That's it. Perfect," she exclaimed, clapping her hands with joy.

Sam and BJ tied the sign off with chains and tightened the main bolts with wrenches.

"You're sure now," Sam asked, exasperated. A fifteen minute job had taken an hour.

"I'm sure," she crooned.

Sam blushed as a couple neighbours drove by, slowing down, and waving at him, puzzled looks on their faces. He prayed he would't wind up the laughingstock of the entire valley.

The sheriff drove by in his SUV, stopped and rolled down the window.

"The Silver Spurs Home for Aging Cowgirls," he said. "That's a good moniker."

"Well, thank you, Sheriff," Emma beamed. "It was Jenny's idea."

"Yeah, cowgirl grandmas, we'll see how well that goes over," Sam mumbled.

"I think you'll do well," Cole replied.

The sheriff stepped out of his 4x4 and walked over to stand by Emma, admiring the fresh sign.

"You know there's a barn dance Saturday night at the Diamond Bar," he remarked, his voice warbling.

"Is that so," Sam kidded him.

"Maybe you'd like to go with me," he said to Emma.

"That would be lovely, Cole, but we have the first of our two ladies arriving on Saturday. I wouldn't be a good host if I just scooted them off to their rooms and took off for a night of dancing," Emma replied smoothly.

Sam guffawed. That was the first he heard of it.

Cole blushed.

"Don't give up on her, young fella," Sam whispered in the sheriff's ear.

Cole grinned.

"Well, maybe another time then," he asked hopefully.

"Definitely, Cole, I'd like that," Emma agreed. "Sorry to cut it short, but we still have a lot of work to do and I have a bucket load of emails to reply too. I had no idea that your suggestion of a retirement home and BJ's idea to make it for old folks who have horses would be such a hit."

"That's good to hear, Emma," Cole muttered, his disappointment showing. "If'n you need any help at all, just call me."

"We got a barn that needs painting," Sam suggested.

"Sam," Emma exclaimed. "The sheriff has more important things to do than paint a barn."

"No, I don't," Cole gushed.

"Wear old clothes," Sam nudged the younger man.

Cole grinned.

"Yes, sir."

The next two weeks were a marathon of work. Sam, BJ, and Cole were sunburnt and exhausted as they climbed down the ladder for the last time. Sam continued to grumble about the colour. It couldn't be 'barn red' like all barns should be, Sam had argued, but no, it had to be some designer colour that Emma thought would look great in photographs.

Sam's back and arms ached. He was too old for this, he realized. Shovelling manure was one thing, painting a two-storey barn was another matter.

If Emma's idea didn't work, Sam knew that at least the ranch would look good when they had to sell it or watch the bank man come to repossess it.

"You gotta admit, Sam," Cole said, "it looks good."

"Why thank-you, Cole," Emma thanked the sheriff as she arrived with three full glasses of lemonade.

"It's a pretty colour," Cole marvelled, stepping back with the others to admire their work.

Sam had to agree with Cole. The old barn did look pretty good. They had painted the outside trim and main beams black. The walls were painted a soft shade of sage green that shone pleasantly under the noonday sun.

"I can't wait to change the pictures up on the website," BJ crooned.

"Now all we have to do is paint the house to match," Emma chirruped.

The men groaned.

The donkey named Mike brayed from his paddock beside the barn.

"You reserve your comments until you learn to pick up a paint brush with your teeth and help out," Sam chastised the donkey.

The donkey hee-hawed loudly: again and again and again.

"Everyone's a critic," Cole joked.

The group gathered around the barn all laughed.

It had taken the last of their savings and then some, but Sam was proud of the result. Maybe this was a wonderful idea.

He wrapped a sweaty arm around Emma's shoulder and hugged her close. She wrinkled her nose, but didn't pull away. Sam chortled.

"I can't believe it," Emma cooed, her gaze fixed on the computer screen.

"What is it," Sam asked, looking over her shoulder.

On the screen, email after email was popping up with questions about the ranch, the daily menu, and amenities. The amount of inquiries had grown daily.

"Tell that broad who wants a pool and a hot tub to move to Florida," Sam said grumpily.

Emma laughed.

"So far, I have two 'definites' and two 'maybes'," she said, her eyes reflecting the beautiful website that her son had drawn up. Shots of the mountains and green pastures filled the page with the stunning vista that the family took for granted every day. The fresh paint made the pictures of the barn with the mountains in the background veritably pop off the screen.

"Who are the two 'definites' moving in on Saturday?" Sam inquired.

Emma grinned, her eyes dancing with mischief.

"Emma," Sam asked again, eyeing her dubiously.

"It's a surprise," she said stubbornly.

"I don't like surprises," he glowered.

"These you will," she chirped.

"Fine," he sulked, "what about the two maybes?"

"They are retired hunter ladies. I've only spoken to one of them because her friend has had a stroke and can't talk," Emma continued. "They seem to have buckets of money and when I Googled them, both women turned out to be really big names in the hunter world. They're pretty too. Look."

Emma started tapping the keyboard, her fingers flying as she typed their names into the Google search engine.

Pictures of two handsome older women mounted on two enormous Warmblood stallions appeared on the computer screen.

"Just make sure they aren't hoity-toity types."

"The woman I talked to was this woman," Emma said, pointing at the slender dark skinned woman mounted on a stunning chestnut stallion. "Her name is Maggie Carroll. This photo is twelve years old, though. She and her friend, Sylvie O'Hara, are quite famous."

"You know my daddy had a saying: *A woman needs two animals—the horse of her dreams and a jackass to pay for it,*" he mused. "We got one jackass in the barn, so let's make sure there won't be any more."

Emma burst out laughing.

"I shall leave it up to you, daughter-dearest," he teased, knowing he had no say in the matter anymore.

"Okay, daddy-o," Emma joked back, exuberantly typing a note to Maggie Carroll telling her they would be happy to welcome Maggie and her friend into their home, not even thinking to ask after the horses.

Captain Hindsight made Sam wish that he was more involved with who came to stay and what kind of baggage they would arrive at the ranch with.

Chapter Three

A young woman is to an old man the horse that he rides to hell.
Spanish Proverb

Saturday arrived. Emma insisted that everyone wear their Sunday best. BJ wore new blue jeans, a checked green and white cotton button-down shirt, and polished-to-a-sheen cowboy boots. Jenny wore a frilly pink dress and sported pink flowers in her hair. She had even braided matching pink ribbons into the donkey's mane, but her mother wouldn't let her bring Mike out to greet the recent arrivals.

Sam sat in his rocking chair. He had refused to wear his going-to-church grey suit, settling instead on clean jeans and a crisp white shirt with a bolo tie festooned with a Navajo jade stone. He had cleaned the scuffs off his boots, but not bothered polishing them. He was a rancher, not a rhinestone cowboy. His white moustache was neatly trimmed, and Emma had given him a fresh buzz cut.

A white-haired woman drove up. Her tiny head was just visible above the steering wheel of the battered old Ford dually she was driving. She pulled the truck and rusted hulk of an angle haul trailer into the yard. The truck bed was loaded with hay.

"Oh, dear," Emma murmured.

"You did say you checked tax records and got first and last month's rent," Sam said, looking pointedly at his daughter-in-law.

"I did," she agreed.

"Has the cheque cleared?"

"Not yet."

Sam guffawed and stood up, hitching up his pants, before striding across the yard to meet the tiny woman who was stepping out of the big pickup truck. Emma and the kids followed along after him.

"Sam Montana, as I live and breathe," the woman gushed as she exited the truck. Curly white hair fell to just above the collar. She wore a denim jacket, comfy jeans, a ruffled cotton blouse, and dust covered western boots that had seen better days. A gold belt buckle with a woman riding a barrel horse sparkled in the sunlight. Deep crow's feet accentuated steel grey eyes. Her smile widened as she walked towards the old rancher.

"Mary Adams, is that you," Sam shouted, jogging forward.

"It is my old friend," she boomed.

Sam lifted her off the ground and spun her in the air.

"Whoa, old man, you'll snap my back faster than a voodoo priestess snapping the neck off a chicken," she said with a laugh.

"I told you I had a surprise for you," Emma chortled.

"You sure did," Sam agreed. "I thought you'd be long since married off and settled down with a bunch of grandkids by now. How long has it been?"

"At least thirty years. Cleve was just a toddler the last time I saw you and Adelaide. I was sorry to hear that she had passed, I know how much you doted on that woman," Mary responded. "Where is Cleve anyway?"

"Cleve died in Iraq five years ago," Emma's voice warbled, a lump rising into her throat.

"He was a hero," Jenny piped in.

"I'm so sorry to hear that, Emma. It never occurred to me to ask when we spoke on the phone. I've been out of the loop for a long time," Mary said, wrapping her arm under Sam's. And then to Jenny, "And who is this pretty peach in front of me, although I can hazard a guess?"

"Jenny," Jenny gushed. "And this is my brother, BJ, and we have a donkey too. I bet you've never met a donkey named Mike before."

Mary laughed.

"No, I can honestly say that I've never met a donkey named Mike."

"Can I help you with your horse, Mrs Adams," BJ asked politely.

"Call me Mary, young man. I've never been a Mrs and don't intend to start now."

BJ blushed. He stood there, arms at his side, not sure what to do.

"Go ahead," Sam motioned towards the trailer, "help the lady with her horse."

BJ jogged around to the back of the trailer as Mary took in the sights.

The dark green mountains glistened beneath the deep blue sky. The pastures were a light green, somewhat wilted from the summer, but the sedge grass around the small creek that ambled through the middle of them was lush and vibrant.

Mary inhaled the clean air.

"Oh, my, this is just how I imagined it," the retired cowgirl said happily.

"What brought you here, Mary," Sam asked, "if it ain't too personal?"

"No, it's not, Sam. I lost my farm in the Florida hurricane last year. Barn blew down. The house was unlivable. The insurance company paid me out, but I just didn't have the heart or the energy to re-build it. I lived in a rented RV on the property ever since."

"You drove all the way from Florida," Emma stuttered, wisely leaving the "in that" left unsaid.

"I did," Mary replied with a grin, knowing exactly what Emma was thinking.

"That's awful. I can't imagine seeing your barn get blowed down," Jenny wailed, pushing her grandfather out of the way and wrapping her arms around the diminutive woman's waist.

A clip-clop clump was heard as BJ led a dark bay and white paint stallion out of the horse trailer. The horse had a white face, two blue eyes, a black mane, black and white tail, and an intelligent elegance about him that spoke to the Thoroughbred side of his Quarter horse heritage. He was tall and solidly built; about sixteen hands.

"He's a beauty," Emma cooed.

"Patch was a champion barrel racer in his day," Mary replied proudly, "and the California State Champion when he was a two-year-old. He's made me a lot of money over his lifetime and has earned a good retirement."

"You still stand him at stud," Sam queried, liking what he saw.

"Only to the right mares," Mary nodded towards her pride and joy. "His back end is a little weak. Like me, my old man has a lot of miles on him."

"How does he feel about donkeys," Emma asked sheepishly.

"Patch's stable mate for twenty years was a donkey," Mary said delightedly. "He's been ever so heartbroken since Beauregard passed away."

"That's wonderful, I mean, not that your donkey died, but that Patch likes donkeys. Patch'll just love Mike then. Mike's uber friendly," Jenny chattered on, grabbing Mary's hand and pulling her towards the barn. "He's real sweet, but I gotta warn you he's real ugly too, what with only one ear and all."

"I'll get your things, Mary," Sam called after the girls.

Mary waved a hand over her head in answer.

"Take Patch into the barn, BJ," Sam instructed his grandson, "and I'll help you unload the hay. Make sure you only give Patch the hay he's used to for tonight. We don't want him to colic."

"Yes, Grandpa," BJ said.

"That must be Mrs Puddicombe," Emma offered, shading her eyes from the sun.

A black BMW turned into the ranch driveway, followed by a horse transport with Minnesota plates.

"Better get that paint stud settled down quick," Sam advised his grandson, "looks like we got more coming."

BJ hurried off with the paint horse in tow as Emma watched the car and horse transport approach.

"And how many horses is this one bringing," Sam asked, raising a questioning eyebrow. "That's a big rig for one horse."

The Beamer pulled up in front of the house and Sam signalled the horse transport driver to pull his eight-horse rig up in front of the barn.

Just then a yellow and white Cessna buzzed over the ranch, so low that it caused Sam and Emma to duck.

"What the….," Sam growled.

"What an idiot," Emma yelped.

The plane flew towards the mountains, its wings wobbling, and a thin stream of blue-black smoke billowing out behind it.

The horses galloped to the barn's gate, fearful of the noise and smell of the burning airplane. The donkey, pink ribbons billowing in the breeze, let out a great big long bray.

"Mom, that plane is on fire," Jenny called from the donkey's paddock. Mary too looked equally as alarmed.

"It's not on fire," Emma returned, "it's just some fool showing off."

"Okay," Jenny said, "but I'm sure I saw flames."

"It wasn't on fire, was it," Emma asked Sam.

"Looks like it's going down," he croaked. "I'll call Cole."

"I didn't expect so much fanfare at my arrival," a short haired woman drawled. She wore black jeans with rose diamante studs on the pockets, a black silk tank shirt, and a tailored black jacket, also studded with rose coloured diamante patterns. Her hair was a mixture of white and black, her blue eyes warm and inviting. She was a handsome woman with an air of confidence.

"Zoe Puddicombe, at your service," the woman said, holding out her hand to first Emma and then to Sam. She fixed Sam with a 100-watt high beam smile. It lit up her entire face.

"Ma'am," Sam replied, tipping his Stetson, his cheeks burning. "I'm Sam Montana."

"So you are," she grinned.

Emma tried to hide her smile behind one hand, but Sam caught her silent laugh and scowled.

"Excuse me, Mrs Puddicombe," Sam said, "but I've got to go call the sheriff. That plane looked in distress."

"So, do you, Mr Montana," Zoe joked. "And please call me Zoe. Mrs Puddicombe is far too formal. It's the worst of my married names, but hopefully it won't be my last."

It startled Sam into silence. For a moment, he forgot what he was about to do.

A muffled 'boom' echoed across the valley. It sounded like a far-off thunderclap.

"That didn't sound good," Zoe gasped.

Sam raced to the house to call the sheriff, leaving the two ladies alone.

"Umm, I'll help you with your bags," Emma ventured, not sure what to do in this situation, what with unfamiliar women and horses arriving at the same time as a small plane crash. Could the day get any weirder?

"That's okay, I'd rather get Zippo and Extravaganza settled in first," she cooed, slipping her arm under Emma's, "and you can tell me more about your delightful father."

Emma blushed.

"He's my father-in-law, actually," Emma confessed.

"And who owns that… shall we say, 'delightful antique rig' over there," Zoe nodded towards Mary's rig.

"Oh, that is Mary Adams's rig. She just got here with her paint stallion, Patch," Emma said, happy to be on firmer ground. "Mary's a retired barrel racer. I'm told she was Queen of the Rodeo for many years."

"That sounds like fun," Zoe bubbled. "I can't wait to meet her. I bet she has some juicy stories."

"I expect she does. I think the two of you will hit it off splendidly," Emma said, warming up to Zoe Puddicombe.

"I know we will."

Sam alerted the sheriff. It niggled him that he hadn't been able to offer to help locate the downed plane, but he had other pressing matters to attend to, like a horse transport unloading who knew what in front of his barn. He would have to talk to Emma later about what kind and how many horses the family were prepared to take in.

He exited the house in time to see the horse box driver and his helper unloading a tall white stallion with a luxurious mane and tail, and an equally stunning grey Andalusian filly. The stallion went ballistic when it caught the scent of the donkey, the filly following suit.

Sam raced across the yard, snatching the stallion's lead rope from the horse handler's hand while the lad was still in the air, his boots two feet above the ground, as the stallion whipped his head straight up and bellowed.

"Easy big guy," Sam crooned to the frightened horse. "Easy, buddy."

The horse handler fell to the ground in a heap and scrabbled out of the way of the stallion's flying hooves.

"Oh, Zippo, settle down," Zoe oozed.

Zoe quietly motioned for Sam to hand over the lead rope.

Sam reluctantly handed the lead rope over, standing close, in case he had to intervene. In Sam's opinion, women didn't belong handling a stud, but it was her horse, so he guessed he'd find out just how good a horse woman Zoe Puddicombe was.

Zoe gently took the stallion's lead rope from Sam as the horse reared and pawed the air with its front hooves once again.

"Don't be so naughty," Zoe said calmly, reaching a hand up to stroke the stallion's neck after he returned to earth.

Sam paled at the thought of BJ or Jenny handling that stud.

"Zippo's just had a lengthy trip. He'll be fine once he settles in," Zoe consoled Sam as the stallion snorted and stood his ground, Zoe's familiar touch and sultry voice calming him instantly.

"Sure, he will," Sam responded dryly, ducking out of the way.

He had to give it to the woman; she handled her stallion with adept coolness, either that or foolhardy bravado.

"That was quite the show," Mary chirped, stopping several paces from the two upset horses. "And a flaming plane and everything."

"You must be the rodeo queen," Zoe remarked dryly, her eyes sparkling with mirth.

"I am," Mary agreed, her eyebrows raising in a questioning look.

"Zippo loves a grand entrance, the filly too, when she's of a mind," Zoe purred.

Mary's paint stallion put his head over his stall door and nickered softly. He then let out an ear-piercing whinny at the introduction of another stallion into the barn.

"That's my Patch," Mary yelled, covering her ears.

"This is Zippo, and the filly is Extravaganza," Zoe proudly announced.

"The filly can go in the stall three doors down," Sam told the transport driver.

The stout driver nodded and led the foaming filly into the barn, her hooves clickity-clacking on the cement floor.

"Just pick a stall for that one," Sam told Zoe, his voice cracking.

Sam glared at Emma as he walked by her, heading up the ladder to the hayloft to throw down some extra hay.

"Two bloody stallions, not just one," he grumbled to himself. "I'm gonna have to build stallion pens now."

Sam had thought he'd seen everything in his day, but he was wrong.

It took an hour for the transport driver and his aid to unload all the tack and horse blankets: night blankets, day blankets, cooling down coolers, summer blankets and fleecy lined winter rugs, two large tack trunks that held two saddles, assorted bridles, brushes, combs and polishes, and then lastly one small trunk to hold the Andalusians trophies and ribbons.

Sam idly wondered how many suitcases that Mrs Puddicombe, make that Zoe, travelled with if this was what her horses required. It didn't bode well.

And then the donkey let out a great bray.

All Hell erupted once again, and Sam didn't have time to think about anything else.

The Montana family sat down to a peaceful dinner after Mike was let loose with the ranch horses. The ranch horses had already become accustomed to the funny one-eared donkey after listening to his midnight cries of loneliness for two weeks. Mike was stabled in a paddock beside the barn. He could see the herd but not interact with them. The wound in his stomach needed time to heal. The vet had just pronounced him healthy enough to go on pasture early that morning, but Sam wanted to wait until after everyone arrived.

"You've really never married," Zoe asked the snowy-haired woman sitting beside her, aghast at such a concept.

"Hell's bells, no," Mary cried out.

Emma gave the old barrel racer a stern look.

Jenny and BJ giggled.

Sam deep dived into his pot roast.

"Oh, my, I am sorry," Mary apologized. "I'm not used to having kids around, especially pretty little girls in pink."

"Or donkey's in pink," Jenny joked.

"That's true too," Mary agreed.

"I've had six husbands, the late Bernie Puddicombe being the last, God rest his soul."

"Six," Emma gasped.

"Heavens, woman, what ever for," Mary cried out. She punctuated the question with a singularly loud gulp of iced tea.

"Well," Zoe replied. "I like men. Mervin was the first. I married him at seventeen. He was my high school sweetheart. I left him at twenty-one when I realized his sole goal in life was to drink beer, fart and watch the Dodgers games over and over again."

Jenny giggled. BJ elbowed her to stop, his face red from trying hard not to laugh.

"My second husband was Jerry. Jerry was a fool, but a rich one, so I did well for myself there. He made the age-old mistake of having an affair with his secretary. My lawyer made mince meat of him. Harry was husband number three. He was ever so handsome. He was an Englishman. Oh, my, but that accent of his was so..."

Emma coughed.

"Marvellously endearing," Zoe finished, catching Emma's pointed look towards the children.

Sam rolled his eyes.

Mary chuckled.

"What happened to Harry," Mary sat forward, intrigued.

"We went rollerblading on the Thames. It was a beautiful sunny day and there were ducks everywhere, even two swans which we stopped to admire. Harry never was an athletic man and well... he stubbed his rollerblade on the tiniest of all cracks in the pavement and tumbled over the wall and into the river. Why he never told me he couldn't swim was beyond me, but... anyway... Thames water isn't the sort of thing one should chugalug. He ended up dying of amoebic dysentery, of all things."

"And number four," Emma asked, also enamoured with Zoe Puddicombe.

"That was Walter. Walter was the oncologist at the hospital who treated Harry. Walter was just a rebound. Our divorce was quite amicable. We realized after a year we had nothing in common, except for extra-curricular activities. If you know what I mean," Zoe grinned salaciously.

Sam guffawed, but remained quiet.

"What is an extra-curricular activity," Jenny asked innocently.

"Volleyball," Mary answered nonchalantly.

Emma, Sam, and Zoe burst out laughing. BJ turned a deep shade of crimson.

"So, when did you get interested in Andalusians," Emma inquired.

"Ah, that was thanks to my fifth husband, Andre." Zoe stopped for a moment, a smile creasing her lips. "My, but I loved that man."

Each person around the table glanced at each other, waiting for her to continue, but she didn't. Instead, she sat there, her eyes vacant, a sad smile on her lips.

"Well," said Sam, using the lull to push his chair back from the table, "we've got a lot of horses to feed."

"Yes, sir," BJ agreed, also pushing away from the dinner table.

"Can I come too," Jenny asked.

"Not yet, Jenny-penny," Sam said, gently cupping her face under the chin with one hand. "I want you to promise me you won't go into either of those stallions' stalls or the filly's until we know more about them."

"Okay, but Mary's horse seems really nice."

"He is a gentle old man," Mary gushed, "but your grandpa is right. Don't you be crawling around in his stall or trying to handle him until your grandpa says it's okay."

"Oh, all right," Jenny moaned.

"Oh, by the way, I heard from Maggie, Sam. They are already on the road. They'll be here first thing in the morning so it will be hectic tomorrow," Emma added shyly, not sure how her father-in-law would react.

"And how many more stallions are they bringing," Sam growled.

"Two," Emma croaked. "I asked."

"Oh, my, four stallions," Mary said, rolling her eyes heavenward. "At least my Patch is quiet. He's twenty-four and has always travelled well. He'd be happy in the paddock with your donkey so don't give him a second thought, Sam."

"That's one good thing," Sam mumbled, retrieving his hat from the hook by the door.

"What about that plane," Jenny asked. "Is Sheriff Cole coming by?"

"I called him. He's out looking for it," Sam assured his granddaughter.

Sam and BJ headed off to care for all the recent arrivals while Emma cleared the plates, Jenny and Mary assisting where they could. Zoe still sat at the table, staring off into space.

Jenny dropped a pan. It clattered to the floor.

"Eek," Mary yelled.

"Ohhh," Zoe gasped, startled out of her reverie. "I guess I drifted off. I was thinking about Andre and well... I guess I just disappeared for a moment."

"Quite all right, Zoe," Mary chirped.

"Where are the boys," Zoe asked, looking around with some puzzlement.

"Gone to the stables to check on our kids," Mary advised her.

"Oh, good," the short haired woman crooned. "Maybe we can join them in a little while."

"I can take you on a tour of the ranch if you want," Jenny piped up.

"That is a lovely idea, young lady," Mary hugged her.

Emma smiled. They may have a lot of testosterone flying around in the barn and whinnying up a storm, but it looked like the ladies would be a great fit with the family.

"You know what I like best," Jenny beamed.

"What is that?" Zoe queried.

"I told mum and grandpa that I only wanted ladies here cuz I wanted some cowgirl grandmas and it looks like I got me two."

Mary and Emma burst out laughing, red faced with glee.

"I must say that I have never been called a cowgirl grandma before," Mary chortled.

"I think I'll go out to the barn and check on my horses," Zoe remarked casually, not quite as impressed as the rodeo queen.

"Not a problem," Emma replied, seeing a flicker of what she thought was revulsion pass over Zoe's face.

"Are you coming, Mary," Zoe asked the wizened cowgirl.

"Maybe a little later," Mary replied. "I think I'll just make myself at home and help Emma clean up."

Emma grinned, pleased.

"Don't you want a tour of the ranch," Jenny pouted.

"In a little while," Mary said, patting the little girl's hand.

"I expect Mary is tired from her lengthy drive," Emma said.

"Can I go with Zoe then," Jenny pleaded with her mother.

"Okay," Emma agreed reluctantly. "You can feed Mike and our herd; maybe give Rosie a brush while you are at it. Don't get in Zoe's or your grandfather's way, and change your clothes first."

"I won't bug them, I promise," Jenny chirruped.

"I'll meet you in the barn, Jenny," Zoe sighed and marched out of the kitchen, a mild look of irritation on her face.

Emma snapped a towel at Jenny's bottom as her daughter raced past.

"Do you think Zoe's okay," Emma asked Mary after Zoe and her daughter were out of ear shot.

"You mean about her drifting off," Mary asked.

"That, among other things," Emma shrugged, non-committed.

"Each of us has our own reasons for coming to stay with you. Time will tell what Zoe's reason is. Mine is because I was tired of being alone and didn't want to spend the rest of my life in a rented RV on my once glorious property. This was the path of least resistance. Zoe is a high stepper, just like those horses and that car of hers. She obviously doesn't enjoy being alone either, or she wouldn't have had all those husbands."

Emma grinned. She liked Mary a lot.

"I also think she's set her sights on Sam."

"Good luck with that," Emma giggled. "Zoe is attractive, but no match for the memory of Adelaide."

"Cheeky."

"Oh, I am terrible."

Mary laughed.

"Wait until I tell BJ and Jenny that he has to move in with his sister," Emma grimaced.

Mary looked quizzically at the lovely woman standing at the sink scrubbing a pot.

"Mrs O'Hara had a stroke. I'm not sure if she can do the stairs, so I'd rather be prepared and fix up a downstairs bedroom for her," Emma explained.

"Ah, the Girl Scout's code, 'always be prepared'," Mary agreed.

"Yep, I'm expecting fireworks tonight," Emma said, returning to the task at hand, "and not from my son."

"Well, it's been that kind of day hasn't it," Mary consoled her.

The two women grinned at each other and then burst into another fit of giggles.

Chapter Four

To ride a horse is to ride the sky.
Author Unknown

Sam was up early. He had let BJ sleep in after his grandson had to move all his belongings up into his sister's room and then listen to the wails of grief from his granddaughter over the horrible indignity of sharing a room with her brother. Oh, the trauma.

Sam chuckled as he moseyed out to the stable, coffee cup in hand.

The morning was cool. A light layer of dew speckled the grass. Pinks and purples dappled the eastern horizon as the sun rose over the dark mountains in the distance. Five ranch horses including Checkers, his flashy sorrel with four white socks and a brilliant blaze on his face, Boomer, his retired roan cutting horse, Penny, Emma's cocoa coloured bay mare, Buckey, BJ's buckskin reining horse, and Rosie, Jenny's naughty pony, plus a one eared donkey named Mike, stood at the gate closest to the barn, looking for their morning grain.

Sam was enormously grateful that the barn was quiet given the horses inside were not used to the ranch routine.

He also appreciated the alone time without Zoe Puddicombe snooping into his personal life and popping up in every nook and cranny. One of his chores today would be to clean out the old outhouse behind the barn. He might need it for a place to hide.

Sam flipped on a light in the barn.

The paint stallion stood up and then snuffled a greeting.

"Good morning, old man," Sam greeted Patch with a rub. The paint horse yawned.

The Andalusian stallion in the stall across the aisle snorted and banged a hoof against the stall door.

"Demanding so and so, aren't you," Sam chuckled, approaching the white stallion. The stallion sniffed him and nickered softly. "Better mood today too, huh?"

The filly two stalls down from the paint stallion whinnied shrilly. She pinned back her ears and half reared inside her stall.

"Yeah, I know, Miss Attitude. I hear you," Sam groaned.

Sam threw a couple of flakes of ranch hay to the two Andalusians. He gave Patch two flakes of the hay that Mary had brought along. He then mixed six buckets full of grain and minerals and took them out to the ranch horses.

He stopped at the gate to examine the donkey and placed the buckets by the fence.

"Now, Mister Mike, you got to learn to behave. You eat from your bucket and not from the others," he scolded the lop-eared donkey.

Mike let out a soft hee-haw.

Sam pushed open the gate and raised his hands, ordering the horses to back off as he retrieved each of the buckets and placed them in front of each of the horses. The pony and the donkey tried to throw their weight around, but neither Sam nor his two cutting horses were having any of it. With a few choice words, Sam handed out all of the buckets and retreated to the other side of the fence.

He watched quietly as the horses and the donkey ate. He never tired of watching the sun rise over the mountain to the east.

He loved this place. The idea that he would be the last of the Montana family to live here didn't sit well with him. He supposed he would just have to get used to all the old hens bustling about, except for Mary. He and Mary shared a lot of history.

With a pang of unimaginable longing, he thought of Adelaide. His heart still ached for her. He fervently wished she were here now. Lord, but it hurt!

Life on the rodeo circuit was hard, but it was never lonely. It was a grand life, not like today, with a world full of fast jets, fast cars, cell phones, computers named after fruit, and apps that he didn't understand. There was no privacy anywhere, except at the ranch… and soon the outhouse.

Sam chortled and then tossed back the last of his coffee. No point living in the past or bitching about today. He retrieved the horse buckets and wandered back to the barn.

He looked at the two-page list of feed requirements that Zoe's horse transport guy had prepared and tacked inside the door to the feed and tack room. He growled in disdain, crumpled the pages up and tossed them in a trash bin.

"Criminy," he muttered to himself.

Sam prepared buckets for the filly and the two stallions. In went sweet feed with oats, soaked beet pulp, and minerals. He made sure that the paint stallion's was good and wet so it wouldn't be too hard for the old man to eat. Sam grinned, wondering when he'd have to eat warm mash for breakfast too.

He placed the buckets on hooks in each of the stalls. The two stallions behaved well, but the filly tried to nip him.

"She's a real mare's mare, isn't she," Mary crooned, startling him. She held a cup of steaming coffee in each hand.

"Oh, Mary," Sam started, wheeling around to face her, "I didn't hear you come in."

"Better clean out your ears, I was humming Dolly's *Coat of Many Colors* as loud as I could without waking the whole ranch up," Mary joked, handing Sam a fresh cup of coffee.

Sam guffawed, accepting the coffee cup with gratitude.

They went to stand in front of Mary's horse's stall to watch her horse eat.

"I'm still an early riser too," Mary said.

"Yep, I never broke the habit, even after the herd was gone," Sam stated huskily.

"Ranching's a hard life."

"So's rodeoing."

"Sure is," Mary agreed. "If you want to turn Patch out in that side paddock, he really will be fine with the donkey or on his own. He doesn't need stud fencing, always been a gentle natured soul," Mary offered.

"That's the impression I got from him," Sam agreed. "He's a nice-looking stud."

"I won Vegas on him four years in a row," Mary said proudly.

"I heard something about that," Sam marvelled. "That's tough competition."

"He could spin on a dime in his day."

"You still ride him?"

"Oh, yes, it does us both good. I don't think I'd do an all-day ride on him anymore, but he's still good for a few hours. I think that's what keeps him going," she said, stroking her horse's velvet nose.

"I'm not surprised," Sam mumbled, glancing down on the top of Mary's head. "You're such a tiny thing, must be like a Barbie doll on top of a bull."

"Sam Montana, I declare," Mary said, slapping him playfully on the arm.

Sam grinned.

The screeching of brakes and the rumble of many vehicles shattered the peaceful morning.

"What in the world is that," Sam jumped, tossing his coffee into the dirt and racing out of the barn, Mary in hot pursuit.

They stopped short at the sight of all the vehicles pulling up in front of the house in a hail storm of dirt and gravel: four black SUV's, the sheriff's SUV, and three state police cruisers.

"Good Lord, are you running a grow-op or smuggling operation, Sam," Mary jested.

Sam shot her an evil look.

"Hey, I'm from Florida," Mary grinned.

The sheriff jumped out of his SUV, trying to head Sam off before he took on the formidable lieutenant of the ATF agents.

Emma, Zoe, and the kids ran out of the house, all of them still in their night robes.

"Goodness look at all these handsome men," Zoe gushed, letting her lacy white gown fall open to reveal the short red silk teddy that she wore underneath it. She smiled and batted her eyes.

"Wish I still had a body like that," Mary crooned, elbowing Sam.

Sam looked at Zoe posing sexually on the porch, her lithe figure, short cropped white hair, and angular face. He rolled his eyes at Mary.

Mary stifled a laugh, her eyes twinkling.

"What's going on," Emma shouted above the hubbub of armed ATF men and state troopers exiting their vehicles.

"Does this have something to do with that plane," Sam yelled at Cole over the din.

"Let's go up to the house," Cole hollered back, pointing towards Emma.

"You better put some more coffee on," Mary called to Emma, "a lot more coffee."

"Emma, get the kids back in the house," Sam ordered his daughter-in-law, alarmed by all the firepower being unloaded from the backs of the vehicles.

Another two trucks pulled in with ATV's in the back of the truck beds and more ATV's on the trailers.

"It is the plane, isn't it," Sam spat at Cole. "Tell me now, before we go in. I don't want my grandchildren scared any more than they are now. Is it smugglers, drug dealers, generally dangerous dudes or what?"

The leader of the ATF crew approached the two men, Mary having retreated into the house with Emma, Zoe and the children.

"Mr Montana, I'm sorry to meet again under these circumstances."

"Gus, good to see you again," Sam greeted the former marine warmly.

"Yes, sir," Gus replied, shaking Sam's outstretched hand.

"I didn't recognize you under your helmet and all that flack gear," Sam drawled, pulling him into a warm embrace.

"You two know each other," Cole gasped.

"The lieutenant served with my son," Sam's voice warbled. "He did good by us."

"Oh," Cole replied, wary of the handsome lieutenant.

Sam noticed Rodriquez sizing up the baby-faced sheriff, his face stiffening perceptibly.

"We have intel that leads us to believe that Tomas Cortez, aka Tommy Cortez, a notorious drug lord and human trafficker was on that plane," Gus told Sam. "He's as dangerous as they get."

"After you called, we choppered out to the crash," Cole jumped in. "We found the pilot. He was dead."

"But Cortez was nowhere to be found," Gus retorted. "The sheriff's team found evidence of a passenger being there in the crash, so we're sure it was Cortez. He's got an army background, so he won't to be easy to find."

"We found boot prints leading away from the crash site, but it got too dark to follow them and whoever it was, Cortez or not, they didn't answer when we hailed them," Cole replied angrily. "And I wasn't about to send my men on a fugitive hunt in the dark."

"Do I need to worry about the women and my grandchildren," Sam asked quickly.

"We're going to set up a base here if you're okay with that, Sam," Gus continued, "and I will make sure you have at least one deputy here at all times."

Sam lifted his Stetson and ran a hand threw his hair.

"But we got more guests coming this afternoon," he growled. "What the heck am I gonna tell them?"

"Don't go riding," Cole suggested.

Sam glared at the sheriff.

Emma opened the front porch door and shouted over the noise, "Coffee's on. I got extra eggs and bacon on too."

She noticed the man chatting to her father-in-law. Recognition dawned on her face. She flew off the porch, her night gown flapping, and leapt into Gus' arms.

Gus' men cheered.

"Gus Rodriquez," Emma gushed. "I didn't recognize you."

Cole's face reddened.

"You look good, Emma," Gus replied innocently.

"Thank you, Gus. I'm doing well better than the last time you were here," Emma continued. "I am so sorry I treated you so poorly after you came all the way from Iraq to see us."

"S'okay, it was to be expected," Gus whispered.

"He came all the way from Iraq," Cole asked softly.

No one answered Cole.

"Your letters after Cleve died touched my heart," Emma continued. "Wait until you see the kids, they've grown some since you were here."

The angular lieutenant stood in full combat gear complete with a bullet-proof vest, helmet, rugged black boots, and a 40 calibre Glock G27 in a case on his hip, looking into Emma's earnest face and blue eyes.

"I expect they have. I'd love to visit after we catch Cortez, but I've got to get going. I would love a coffee to go," Gus stammered.

Sam saw Cole's face redden even more when he realized just who the ATF lieutenant was.

"What about you, Cole," Sam asked the sheriff. "Have you and your men eaten?"

"Yes, thank you," Cole murmured. "Coffee would be good though."

"Emma, how about Mary and I fetch the coffee for these boys while you go in the house and get dressed," Sam suggested.

Emma looked down at her skimpy cotton nightdress with the picture of a cute Pug blowing heart shaped kisses on the front of it. She blushed redder than a rose in bloom.

She spun on her bare feet and raced back into the house, calling over her shoulder, "We'll catch up later, Gus."

Cole stewed while Gus grinned, watching Emma's priceless retreat.

"Uh, hum, Lieutenant, don't forget that is my daughter-in-law," Sam growled.

"Yes, sir," Gus saluted.

Sam slapped him good-naturedly on the back.

"All right get those bush buggies unloaded and then lock and load," Gus ordered his men.

The state troopers stood still, arms at their sides, looking to Cole for guidance.

"You guys too," Cole ordered his men.

Two troopers giggled until they saw the deadly look on Cole's face.

Sam let the paint out into the side paddock and watched him buck his way across the dirt expanse, happy to be free of travelling. He tossed a few flakes of Florida hay and a couple flakes of ranch grown orchard grass into the paddock while BJ filled up all the water troughs.

"We'll put Mike in with Patch later," he shouted to his grandson. "I don't want him spooking the stallion or the filly when we let them have a romp in the riding ring."

"Okay, Grandpa," BJ waved, moving on to the next water trough.

"I'm gonna put the stallion out first," Sam added. "Hopefully, he won't jump the rails."

"That won't be necessary," Zoe piped up, walking towards him. "I'll lunge him first and ride him in the ring for a while."

"You sure," Sam asked, shocked. "He'll be frisky."

"I like my men frisky," she teased, heading back to the barn, her form fitting black riding breaches hugging her figure, her leather riding boots spit polished, pale pink blouse leaving nothing to the imagination, and a black felt helmet under one arm.

Sam exhaled the breath he didn't realize he was holding. He would definitely have to brush the cobwebs out of the outhouse this afternoon.

BJ left the water hose tucked deep inside the pasture's trough and walked over to where his grandfather was standing admiring the newcomer. With a loud grunt, his granddad switched his attention back to the paint stallion, and the giant bucks the paint was letting out as he spun and galloped back and forth across the paddock, snorting with happiness.

"She's a bit crazy, isn't she," BJ whispered, nodding towards the spot where Zoe had just been standing.

"As a loon, I'm thinking," Sam agreed.

"She's awfully pretty though," BJ stammered, "I mean for a lady her age."

"Mind your manners, boy," Sam guffawed. "And the trough is over-flowing.

BJ saw the water spilling out over the water trough and ran to grab the hose.

Sam chuckled under his breath and went to check the sand ring's footing and fences. Last thing he needed was a lawsuit by one crazy old hen.

The riding ring was large. The footing was sand. BJ kept it up as he liked to practice on the big buckskin gelding.

Every so often, Sam asked one of their neighbours to bring a few cows over for BJ to practice on. The kid had a real knack for it, but was staying quiet about which college he wanted to go to and what subject he wanted to major in. Sam couldn't help but respect him for that. It was BJ's choice, not his grandfather's or his mother's.

Sam made sure the long narrow wood railed cattle chute at the end of the ring was gated off.

The fence around the ring was wood railings. It was almost six feet high and was solid of beam. They used the arena for cattle branding and sorting when they had cattle. The last thing they wanted was injuries to horse, cow, or human.

Sam spotted a loose wire and pulled a pair of pliers from his back pocket. He re-wrapped the wire and tucked it snugly under a wood rail.

A loud whinny split the air. It was so high pitched, it hurt the ears.

Sam turned and saw Zoe leading her prancing stallion towards the ring. An elegant black leather dressage saddle sat on his back. A stallion chain wrapped over his nose and then tucked through the ring under his leather halter helped keep him in control. She held a long dressage whip in one hand and tapped it on the ground beside him whenever he crowded her space.

The stallion danced on the spot, his tail held high in the air, his eyes bright and alert.

Zoe walked calmly beside him, urging him forward quietly with the touch of a hand and a whisper in his ear.

Sam was impressed. He might think her a little bonkers, but the lady could handle a stud. That Spanish husband of hers must have taught her well.

"BJ be a darling and run me out the lunge line and bridle I left on the door hooks beside Zippo's stall," Zoe asked the boy.

"Yes, ma'am," BJ yelled, racing off to do the lady's bidding.

"I don't suppose you need any help," Sam drawled, opening the gate for her.

"No, thank-you," Zoe replied charmingly, leading the stallion into the ring.

"I must say that horse of yours is a looker."

"Yes, he is," Zoe grinned.

Sam shut the gate and leaned against it, ever watchful.

BJ returned with the lunge line and a black leather bridle with double reins. He handed them to her through the fence.

Zoe slipped off the stallion chain and slipped on the lunge line. The horse tried to bolt away from her, but she flicked the whip towards his quarters without touching him and drove his hind quarters towards the fence. The horse snorted and stood there quietly.

Sam whistled under his breath.

Zoe winked at him and then worked her stallion in a circle. He bucked and reared on the circle pattern as she drove him subtly from one end of the ring to the other in ever larger circles, letting him play, but not allowing him to bolt or drift out from the pattern.

Mary and Emma came out to watch. Behind them, they could hear the filly screaming and tearing up her stall.

"BJ, bring Rosie in and put her in a stall beside the filly to keep her from fretting," Sam ordered his grandson.

BJ's gaze never left the magical show of horsemanship that was unfolding in front of him. The stallion's white coat sparkled under the sunlight as he leapt into the air, his mane and tail billowing in the wind in a tidal wave of silken threads.

"Now!"

BJ ran across the farmyard, grabbed a rope halter off the fence and raced across the pasture as fast as his legs would carry him.

"That is a magnificent display of horsemanship," Mary said, awestruck.

"It is," Sam agreed, breathless.

BJ returned with Rosie and trotted her into the barn. The ruckus in the barn stopped immediately.

"Where's Jenny," Sam asked his daughter-in-law.

"Entertaining the deputy that Cole left to keep us company," Emma said, her eyes fixed on Zoe and her Andalusian stallion.

Zoe walked towards them, the stallion walking proudly beside her, eyes alert, nostrils flared.

"Who's a wonderful boy," she purred, scratching the horse under his mane. The stallion leaned in towards her hand.

Zoe smiled at her audience as if she was used to the adoration and slipped off the halter. She slipped the bit into the stallion's mouth and pulled the bridle over his head.

"Do give me a leg up will you, Sam," she purred.

Sam climbed over the rails and clasped his hands together so that Zoe could step up into the stirrup.

Zoe smiled a thanks as she mounted and then took up the reins and rode off, leaving everyone at the fence to gape at the myriad of manoeuvres she completed on the graceful horse.

"Oh, I forgot," Emma said breathlessly, "Maggie and Sylvie will be here within the hour."

"That's nice," Sam replied, entrenched in Zoe's performance.

"Do you think she'll give me lessons," BJ blurted out. "I'd love to learn to ride like that."

"It couldn't hurt to ask," Mary said.

Sam watched, as awestruck as the rest. Mary slipped an arm under his.

"You aren't falling for her, are you," Mary whispered in his ear. "I think this show is for you."

Sam harrumphed.

Mary chuckled.

"Ooooh, Sam Montana," she said even more quietly. "That woman will eat you alive."

"You know what Roy Rogers used to say, 'When you're young and you fall off a horse, you may break something. When you're my age, you splatter.'" Sam replied.

Mary roared with laughter.

Chapter Five

Quiet horses kick the hardest.
Armenian Proverb

Emma sat with Mary and Zoe on the front porch, all of them quietly rocking and drinking tea, enjoying the warm summer rays and the view of the horses in the fields, the blue-green mountains, and the big sky above.

Propped against the wall behind her was a loaded Remington twelve-gauge shotgun in case Mr Cortez found his way to the ranch.

Sam had mumbled about working on some project or other behind the barn, and she had watched his lean figure stalk off like a feral cat.

She had sent BJ off with the deputy to talk to the neighbours about the downed plane and the possible fugitive at large. She and Sam between them had called everybody they could think of, but most folks thought they were pulling their legs and didn't believe them. The sheriff's deputy should silence the disbelievers, she reasoned. If they needed more convincing, they could

65

check out their front yard: four black SUV's, the sheriff's Suburban, two deputy cars and four state police vehicles and trailers stood in a long line at the side of the house.

Jenny sang away in the living room. She was working on her song, bound and determined to put on a show for the cowgirl grandmas this evening. Emma chewed on her lower lip. She was more nervous about her daughter's show than the renegade drug smuggler roaming the hills.

A large one-ton white Chevy pickup truck pulled into the drive pulling a Cadillac of a matching white four horse trailer with a separate living compartment in the front. Emma whistled. She had seen pictures of these rigs in the horse magazines but had never imagined that she'd see one up close.

"Looks like your two new cowgirl grannies have arrived," Mary joked.

"Hmmm, and they have money too," Zoe whispered before taking a sip of Earl Grey tea. She put the cup back down, her eyes narrowing as she watched the enormous rig approach.

Emma waved the driver pulled in. He was a ruddy faced older man, the top of his bald head gleaming as he rolled down the window and leaned forward to wave back. Beside him sat a beautiful woman with cocoa coloured skin and shiny black hair peppered with white at the temples. What looked like a frail auburn and silver haired woman sat in the back seat staring vacantly out the truck's window.

Emma blanched. She knew that Sylvie O'Hara had a stroke and was in a wheelchair, but she didn't think she would be a complete invalid. They weren't prepared to handle that.

Chin up, Emma chided herself. The ladies can afford the care. In a year the family debts will be clear and the ranch's bank accounts will be in the black.

"Hello," she called to the driver.

"You must be Emma Montana," the man yelled in a pleasant baritone.

"I am," Emma confirmed. "If you pull up to the barn, my father-in-law will come out and help you with the horses. My son isn't here, but he'll be back shortly, and we can bring in the ladies' luggage."

"Right-o," the man replied brightly.

The Chevy pulled forward, angling the trailer in so it would be easier to unload the two horses within it. The man parked the long rig with an expert grace.

Maggie Carroll stepped out of the truck and looked around. Her lips, though luscious and round, grew taught, pinching her face into a scowl.

"That doesn't bode well," Zoe murmured from her end zone seat on the front porch.

"I have to agree with you there, Mrs Puddicombe," Mary concurred, her voice so low it was barely audible.

The driver gambolled out of the cab, a wide, earnest grin on his face. The sun bounced off his bald pallet, his shoulder length wisps of white hair lifting comically in the breeze, reminiscent of one of those fuzzy brooms one uses to sweep the cobwebs off a ceiling fan.

"He looks nice," Zoe said. "He handles that rig well. Maybe you should go introduce yourself."

"I think not," Mary guffawed.

"I didn't mean it as an insult," Zoe chortled, amused.

"I know. Not my type, but thank you for the thought," Mary warbled.

"A woman has needs."

"Not since menopause," Mary glowered.

"You must admit, he has a lovely smile," Zoe giggled.

"Mrs Puddicombe, you are incorrigible," Mary replied smoothly.

"You can't tell me you wouldn't like to have the cobwebs dusted out every so often," Zoe answered cheerily. "Come on, admit it. That Sam Montana is a striking man."

"And here I was thinking you were talking about that driver."

"I was, but now I'm not," Zoe teased.

"Sam Montana lives for the memory of his wife and his family. You'll do well to remember that. The road you're on will only lead to disappointment, trust me."

"I like a challenge," Zoe quipped.

Mary shook her head and refilled her tea cup.

The two women watched placidly as the driver opened the Chevy's rear door while the black-haired woman wheeled a wheelchair around from the far side of the one-ton truck. The driver carefully lifted the auburn-haired woman out of the back seat and placed her in the wheelchair. He grabbed a throw rug and tucked it gently around her hips and then fastened a seat belt around her stomach, so she didn't slip out of the chair.

"I don't think our Emma was prepared for that," Mary muttered.

"Poor Sam," Zoe sympathized.

Mary rolled her eyes in disbelief.

"Where is he anyway," Zoe asked, leaning forward.

"He's coming now," Mary noted as Sam walked out of the barn and pushed his hat back on his head, a habit he had when something puzzled him.

The ladies watched him shake hands with the driver and then introduce himself to Maggie and to the woman who stared off into space as if she heard and saw nothing. Sam's face flushed at the latter.

The driver motioned towards the side door of the horse trailer and the two men went about unloading the horses as Emma chatted quietly with Maggie, their words soft and muffled.

"I bet she's asking about the police cars," Mary mused watching the dark skinned woman's face grow even gloomier. "Doesn't look happy, does she?"

"This is better than a soap opera," Zoe chirped happily.

Emma pointed to the house and to the two women sitting on the porch.

"Smile," Mary quipped, waving a hand at the raven-haired woman.

Zoe lifted a hand and did her best Queen's wave, hand cupped, fingers tight together, rotating first right and then left.

"Looks like you've got some competition," Mary rejoiced.

"That's not competition, darling, that's a Mexican blackbird," Zoe said, fluffing her hair and pinching her cheeks.

Mary roared with laughter.

"Oooohhhh, meow. The gauntlet has been thrown," Mary chortled.

"What's a Mexican black bird," Jenny asked, bolting onto the porch.

The two women glanced at each other, their faces stricken.

"Wow look at those horses! I love that flashy chestnut. Oh, no I don't, check out the dapples on that bay," Jenny gasped, forgetting her question as her eyes grew wide with curiosity.

Jenny raced off the porch and across the yard, skidding to a stop beside her mother as her grandfather and the driver unloaded the two Warmblood stallions. A crystal breaking whinny erupted from the chestnut stallion while the dark bay stood quietly looking around at his new surroundings.

The donkey and the herd of Quarter horses jogged to the fence line and hung their heads over top of the wood rails, eyeing the newcomers.

Sam led the tall Hanoverian into the barn. The stallion walked calmly past the herd of ranch horses, raised his tail, cut wind, and dumped a giant wad of manure behind him to mark his grand entrance.

Yet another ear-splitting bellow issued from the chestnut stallion as the horse box driver tugged on the stallion's chain. The horse shook his head and tried to rear, but his handler was having none of it and drove him forward, letting out the line only long enough to keep the horse from bolting up the Hanovarian's rear end.

"Well, that's a fine howdy-doody," Mary said, the creases around her eyes deepening as she fought back the giggles.

"I've seen that chestnut before. That's Desert Storm, I do believe. He's a Trakehner stallion. Impressive, I must say."

"You know him," Mary inquired, eyebrows lifting.

"Yes. My late husband, Bernie, was a jump rider. He wanted to breed Desert Storm to one of his mares. He was about to make the arrangements when he died at Hampton Park trying to stop a runaway horse," Zoey said, her eyes misting over.

"I heard about that," Mary gasped. "That was your husband?"

"Yes, it was. I was at the Andalusian sale in Vegas. The officials told me he saved countless people that day," Zoe sighed wistfully. "Typical Bernie."

"I'm so sorry, Zoe," Mary said, leaning over to pat Zoe's hand.

"Thank you," Zoe replied woodenly.

"I guess we should go introduce ourselves," Mary replied after a moment.

"They'll come to us," Zoe responded softly.

The one eared donkey at the fence let out his usual long winded heeee-haaaaaa, and the chestnut stallion called Desert Storm leapt into the air like a Halloween cat.

Emma watched her father-in-law and the horse transport driver lead the two stallions towards the barn. She was glad that the hammer-headed bay was happy simply to be lead forward as if it was just another day of showing. The bay towered over her father-in-law. The chestnut was high-strung and flashy, a typical red head, flighty and emotional. His reaction's to Mike's welcome was something to behold.

"I've never seen a horse jump straight up like that before," Jenny gushed.

Jenny clung to Emma's hand, the vibrations that travelled through every nerve in her little body translating into tremors the like of which would split a continent in two.

At the last minute, the chestnut stallion snorted and bolted after his travelling companion. The transport driver held on to the chestnut's lead rope for dear life as the horse carried him into the barn behind Sam and the bay. The pair disappeared into the darkness with a clatter of hooves and a loud shriek.

"Don't let Storm get away from you, Cade," Maggie yelled at the transport driver.

"It's all good," the man inside the barn shouted.

"Mum, I finished it," the little red-haired girl said animatedly.

"Shhh, honey, Mrs Carroll is talking," Emma chastised her daughter.

"Not the arrival I expected. Armed troops. Donkeys. Is there anything else I should know about other than that we have an armed trooper in the house and a murderer on the loose in the hills," Maggie demanded, one hand on the arm of her friend's wheelchair.

"No one said he was a murderer," Emma back peddled. "A smuggler and drug runner is what we were told."

"Then why do you have a shotgun propped against the wall of the house," Maggie observed.

"Snakes," Jenny offered.

Maggie gasped, her eyes widening in horror.

Emma thought the well appointed and perfectly manicured woman with flawless skin, designer jacket and suede boots, would faint. She hadn't seen a woman swoon before but assumed that this was what it would look like.

The handicapped woman in front of Maggie began to quake.

"Oh my gosh, your friend is shaking," Emma stuttered, alarmed. "Jenny, run and get that Navajo blanket from the couch in the living room and bring it out here."

"Lickety-split," the precocious girl shouted and raced back to the house.

"Really, there is nothing to worry about," Emma consoled her. "The sheriff is a friend of ours, and the lieutenant in charge of the ATF unit is more than capable of handling this Tommy Cortez fellow. The lieutenant's a former marine. He was part of my husband's unit in Iraq."

"That doesn't bode well, does it," the dark-haired older woman said callously.

"Why," Emma asked, puzzled.

"Well, didn't you say you were a widow?"

"Yes, I lost my husband in combat five years ago."

"Then he didn't do a splendid job at protecting him, did he," Maggie barked coldly.

Emma inhaled sharply. What a cruel thing to say.

Jenny returned with the blanket.

Emma ground her teeth, fighting back the retort that sprung to her lips, not wanting to say something she'd regret in front of her daughter. The urge to tell the woman to load her friend and their two damned stallions back into the horse trailer and get off their property was overwhelming, but they were here and that was that.

Jenny wrapped the blanket tenderly around Sylvie O'Hara's shoulders. Instinctively, she hugged the wheelchair bound woman and whispered in her ear, "Don't worry, I'll protect you, and really I was only kidding about the snakes. We have snakes, but they're only itty-bitty ones."

Emma saw the woman's eyes crinkle with mirth. Sylvie reminded Emma of Annie Potts, the mother-in-law on the *Young Sheldon* television series.

So, Sylvie O'Hara couldn't speak and had difficulty focusing, but she definitely understood everything that was being said to her. That heartened Emma's soul.

Sam and the horse transport driver walked out of the barn. Her father-in-law was grinning at something the man had said.

"So, Emma, meet Cade O'Hara, Sylvie's husband," Sam smirked.

Emma blanched.

"What?"

"Yep, old Cade here was telling me how much he was looking forward to riding in the mountains on one of our ranch horses," Sam chortled, glowering at Emma. "He's a real funny guy."

Cade beamed, not understanding the undertones of Sam's statement.

Oh, no, Emma fumed. No one said anything about a husband tagging along with the two women. There was only a single bed in the downstairs room. It had been BJ's. It wasn't necessary to add another bed into Jenny's room as it already had a bunk bed. Now, they would have to drag BJ's bed upstairs into her bedroom and drag hers and her husband's queen sized bed downstairs into the extra bedroom they had set up for Sylvie.

Sam looked her dead square in the eye.

Emma knew exactly what he was thinking: this was all her fault!

Chapter Six

Horses are predictably unpredictable and so are donkeys.

Sam and BJ stood in the doorway of the tiny tack room. Their arms were full of horse blankets. Sam dropped his blankets on the floor.

"They're all crazy, BJ," Sam muttered to his grandson.

"Yes, sir," BJ mumbled back.

Between the Montana family's five western saddles, Mary's barrel racing saddle and western trail saddle, Zoe's two dressage saddles, the Montana family grooming bucket, Mary's small tack trunk, Zoe's two enormous tack trunks, and Zoe's horses countless blankets, there wasn't an empty square foot in the tack room.

"What are we gonna do, Grandpa?"

"Hell if I know," Sam grumbled.

Sam strolled up and down the big barn, thinking on what to do.

The barn had five box stalls and three standing stalls on the south side of the barn, and three box stalls and one standing stall on the north side of the barn. The south side also had a storage area that they used for wheelbarrows, hand tools, pitchforks, and a small John Deere tractor that they used for general cleanup, snowploughing the drive in the winter and floating the riding ring. The large John Deere and haying equipment was stored separately on the property. The tack room, feed bins, and a hay storage area were also on the north side of the barn.

Patch, Zippo and Midnight Special were stabled in the box stalls on the south side of the barn and Extravaganza and Desert Storm were on the north side. That left two box stalls for Checkers and Boomer to use between the three stallions since the Quarter horses were geldings and wouldn't cause a ruckus with the stallions. That left three standing stalls for Penny and Rosie, Emma's and Jenny's horses, and Mike the one eared donkey. He would stable Bucky between the Andalusian filly and the other stallion once the weather got bad.

Sam smiled, pleased with himself.

BJ stood patiently; his arms stuffed full of a huge fluffy purple winter blanket.

"This is what we're gonna do," Sam beamed, returning to his grandson. "We're gonna drag all those damnable horse blankets down to the last standing stall. We'll pound some nails into the cross beams and hang 'em all up so they're off the floor. That'll free up a whole mess of space."

"What about the show blankets, the fancy ones," BJ asked, his arms sagging from the weight of the winter blanket. "The ladies will be madder than hornets if we mess with those."

"Yeah, you're right. We'll leave those in the tack room."

"Take that darn thing and drop it down there," Sam ordered BJ, pointing to the last stall on his left, "and I'll go fetch a hammer and some large stud nails."

BJ waddled down the aisle, his arms rebelling at the weight of the extra-large rug. The bay, chestnut and white stallions watched him with interest, quietly munching away on hay in their stalls. Patch and the grey filly were outside on turn-out.

"You guys better appreciate this," BJ mumbled to the horses as he walked by.

Sam chuckled as he watched his grandson work. The boy looked so much like his father at that age that sometimes Sam couldn't breathe, his heart constricting in his chest, with the pain of loss.

Sam smoothed down his moustache and sauntered to the back of the barn where he kept several buckets full of nails and another bucket of tools.

He heard the roar of an ATV and did an about face, heading to the door to see who was returning.

The sheriff rode up on one of the ATVs. A dark-haired girl in a Forestry Service Ranger's uniform cantered along beside him on a big bay Quarter horse. They stopped at the eight-foot wide gate that led out to the ranch's farthest hay pasture.

Sam met them at the gate.

"How ya doing, Dee," Sam said to the youthful woman astride the stout gelding.

"Long time no see, Mr Montana," the Ranger drawled.

"You gotta stop being a stranger, is all," Sam quipped. "Emma'll be thrilled to see you."

The girl's broad smile lit up her face. Dee Gallant was an angelic woman with delicate features, big brown eyes, black auburn hair that fell well past her broad shoulders, and a soft voice that made animals feel safe and a man's heart go pitter-patter. While her features made her appear diminutive, her frame was womanly and strong, her character one of fierce determination. She was also an expert tracker.

"I'm guessing you haven't caught him yet," Sam said to Cole while he opened the gate for the ATV and horse to go through.

"No, sir, not a sign of him," Cole replied before gunning the ATV and barrelling through the gate.

Dee followed him.

Sam closed and locked the gate before following the two into the yard.

Cole turned off the ATV and dismounted, taking off his helmet as he did so.

"My deputy staying out of the way," Cole asked the old cowboy.

"Yep, Jenny's keeping him entertained," Sam grinned. "I think she's got a small crush on the young fella."

Cole laughed.

Dee dismounted and patted her gelding on the neck. The horse's dapples were invisible under the coat of dust that turned the sweat on his chest and haunches into muddy ringlets of grey brown.

BJ raced out of the barn and skidded to a stop. He turned a deep shade of red when he saw Dee.

"Can I help you with your horse, Miss Gallant," he gushed. "Looks like you had to ride him hard today."

Sam tucked his head into his chin to hide a smile. It seemed like his granddaughter wasn't the only one who had a crush.

"Thanks, but I need to head home," Dee said, "although I guess he could use a little walk and some water. It's been a long-haul."

"Why don't you let BJ tend to him and come on in the house? We got room. Emma cooked a turkey as big as Texas. You can save me from having to eat turkey the rest of the week," Sam offered.

Cole and Dee laughed.

Dee pushed the hair from her face with one hand and handed BJ the reins with the other.

"I can't say 'no' to that," Dee warbled, her voice sweet as a jay bird.

BJ blushed even darker as he took the reins from her hand.

Sam thought his grandson's knees would buckle.

"Looks like the last of your guests have arrived," Cole said, nodding towards the O'Hara's truck and trailer. "That is some rig."

"Yep, it comes complete with a joker named Cade and a harpy by the name of Maggie Carroll," Sam growled, deciding not to mention the handicapped wife.

"That doesn't sound good," Cole replied, worriedly.

"I wouldn't worry about 'em," Sam chortled. "I don't think they'll stay for long."

"Don't expect the sight of all the cop cars helped," Dee added. She whistled as she looked over all the vehicles that cluttered the ranch yard.

"Expect so," Sam nodded.

"BJ, come up to the house after you've looked after Dee's horse and wash up for dinner," Sam called to his grandson.

BJ had already unsaddled the bay gelding in front of the outside tap, making ready to give him a wash down with a hose to remove the trail dust and cool him off.

"Okay. Where do you want me to put him once I've washed him down?" BJ hollered back.

"Put him in the box stall beside that grey filly's and give him a couple sheaves of hay and some water," Sam yelled.

BJ nodded and continued to work on the tired horse. The gelding snuffled the boy's pockets as he rubbed him down.

"I think you have a fan," Sam whispered to Dee as the three of them walked up to the house.

Dee grinned.

"Let him down lightly, Dee," Cole joked, his eyes twinkling with mirth.

"What makes you think I'll let him down," Dee replied casually. "He's handsome like his father. Maybe I'm willing to wait a few years."

Sam guffawed and held the door open for her.

The Montana family home was enormous and rambling, but like many a ranch home, the soul of the house was in the kitchen.

The kitchen was warm and welcoming. An old black iron woodstove stood against one wall with two sticks of firewood piled against it, ever ready for a power outage. The stove was big and modern, propane fuelled. Emma had bought it with Mary and Zoe's deposit cheques, not wanting their old stove to die on them right when she had to cook for so many.

Food galore filled the kitchen counters. A thirty-pound turkey sat cooling beneath tin foil. There were two bowls of mashed potatoes, two cups filled with gravy, a giant bowl of Emma's apple and sage stuffing, a bowl of candied carrots, broccoli, homemade bread, and two apple pies for dessert.

Jenny sat at the table between Mary and a cherub-faced deputy. She wore her Sunday-go-to-church lilac coloured dress. Zoe sat beside Mary, an amused expression on her face. Across from them, a pinch-faced Maggie sat beside a flush-faced Cade. Sylvie sat in her wheelchair on the far side of Cade. Cade fastened a cloth bib under his wife's chin. They all looked up as Sam, Dee and Cole entered the kitchen.

"Goodness, that turkey smells divine," Dee gushed as she stepped through the doorway.

"Heaven on earth," Cole agreed.

"Dee," Emma squealed with delight, flying across the kitchen, apron flapping, cheeks flushed. She wrapped her arms around her friend and gave her an enormous bear hug.

"If you're gonna cook like this every day, I'm gonna start stopping by more often," Dee giggled.

"Any time, my friend," Emma replied, releasing the Ranger.

"Jenny, fetch another two chairs from the living room," Sam said, taking a seat at the head of the table.

"I'll get the settings," Mary offered, rising from her spot.

Jenny jumped up and raced to the living room, dragging in first one and then another antique wooden rail chair.

"We don't want to put you out," Cole said, hat in hand, noticing the full table.

"You aren't putting us out at all, Cole," Emma beamed.

"That's good," Cole replied. "Right now, I know there's a whole lot of ATF agents and deputies who wish they were here."

"Are they coming in soon," Emma asked, returning to the kitchen counter and picking up a wet stone. She began sharpening the carving knife. The sound of metal grinding on stone was grating.

"Those boys are prepared for Armageddon," Dee chortled.

"They're camping out on the mountain," Cole added.

"They're sure determined to catch this guy," Sam said.

"How dangerous is he really," Cade asked. "The deputy told us he's one of America's Most Wanted."

"Cortez is a bad 'un from what Lieutenant Rodriguez told us. Did time south of the border, broke out of a maximum-security prison twice. He's one nasty piece of work," Cole continued, taking a seat at the table.

"He's got some tracking background; I can tell you that. I lost him in that dry gulch below Dead Horse Pass," Dee added, taking a seat beside Cole. "He covered his tracks really well."

"Mum's got her shotgun loaded and ready by the stove, so I'm not scared," Jenny quipped, skipping through the kitchen to help her mother dish out the scrumptious meal.

"Nothing scarier than a momma bear protecting her young," Sam chortled.

"Can I help you, Emma," Cole asked casually, his eyes as big as a puppy dog's as he watched Emma bustling about.

Dee blushed and knotted her hands together beneath the table.

Sam noticed the interaction. Could Dee be sweet on Sheriff Trane? If so, that would be awkward. Cole couldn't have broadcast his feelings for Emma any louder if he had shouted it to the heavens or had a plane sky write it over the ranch. Throw in a rugged marine named Gus Rodriquez and a dangerous fugitive, fireworks were bound to happen. Some interesting times were ahead at the Montana Ranch.

"How exciting," Cade declared. "I might have to go into town and buy a cowboy hat just like yours, Sam."

"Might you now," Sam snorted.

"Grandpa will teach you how to cowboy Mr Cade, won't you, Grandpa?"

"Um, that's Mr O'Hara, sweetheart, but you can call me plain ole Cade," the old man grinned.

"But that isn't respectful, Mr Cade, er, Mr O'Hara," the girl twittered. "I just can't do that. It wouldn't be right."

Dee stopped wringing her hands and smothered a laugh as everyone at the table giggled, all except for Cade's wife and Maggie.

"I'm not sure if I should serve everyone from here or just plop everything down on the table for you folks to serve yourselves," Emma moaned, a spoonful of mashed potatoes in her hand.

"I think except for Mrs O'Hara, we can all serve ourselves," Sam replied, putting an end to the matter.

"Indubitably," offered Cade.

"What's that mean," Jenny chirped.

"Without a doubt," Cade answered.

"That's a delightful word… indubitable," Jenny cried out.

"Indubitably," Mary, Emma and Zoe said together.

"Well, I would prefer to be served, but that is entirely up to you, Mrs Montana," Maggie purred like a panther stretching its talons.

Sam was indignant. He opened his mouth to say something when Emma beat him to it.

"We plan on this being a happy household filled with love and support, Mrs Carroll. Here, majority rules," Emma barked, depositing a bowl of mashed potatoes down on the table in front of Maggie with a loud 'thunk,'.

Good for Emma, Sam mused, a sly grin creeping across his face.

"Be civil, dear," Cade said, gently patting Maggie's hand.

The intimacy of the gesture startled Sam. Was Sam missing something? Wasn't Sylvie Cade's wife?

He saw Zoe and Mary exchange a wizened look.

"I can't wait to dig into that turkey," Cole gushed, not noticing the tension that had suddenly filled the room.

"And I can't wait for my first cowboy lesson," Cade grinned as Emma placed a simple clay plate down on the table in front of him. "And don't worry about my wife, Emma, I'll take care of her the same as I have always done. You either, Sam, I'll deal with her dressing and bathing. I've been doing it for five years and plan on doing it until she finally recovers from this horrid stroke."

"That's good of you," Zoe chirped.

"I love my wife, Mrs Puddicombe, we've been through Hell and high water as they say and here we are, still together after forty-five years," Cade said proudly.

Sylvie winced, her eyes flashing dangerously, but quickly recovered.

Sam saw it.

He would have to keep an eye on Cade O'Hara. There was something fishy going on and Sam didn't like it, not one little bit.

"Is that why you came here," Emma inquired as she and her daughter deposited the bowls of food at intervals on the long trestle table.

"Yes, ma'am, it is. We, that is, me and Maggie, hope that the fresh mountain air and life at the ranch will help my Sylvie recover."

Maggie glowered at her empty plate, remaining silent as she did so.

"Mrs O'Hara must mean a lot to you," Mary said to the unhappy woman across the table from her.

"Ow," Mary griped, reaching down to rub her shin where Zoe had kicked her under the table.

Zoe gave her a warning look.

"Sylvie and I are childhood friends," Maggie offered, lifting her chin. "We spent years competing against each other and are the better for it."

"Still are, I bet," Zoe mumbled.

It was Mary's turn to nudge Zoe under the table. Zoe shrugged.

"You are a dutiful husband, Cade," Mary crooned.

Zoe rolled her eyes.

Trust the ladies to know exactly what kind of man he and Emma had just let into their home, Sam thought.

BJ burst into the house.

"Hope you haven't started without me. I'm as hungry as a mountain lion," he called, racing over to the sink to wash his hands before sitting down.

"We haven't. Sit down, BJ, then we'll say grace," BJ's mother said, handing him a towel.

BJ wiped his hands, grinned, and plopped himself down in the last remaining seat at the table. He stared wide eyed at Dee sitting demurely across the table from him.

Sam chuckled and steepled his hands together above the dinner table, leaning slightly forward to make a point when he saw Cade and Maggie not doing the same as everyone else. Sylvie O'Hara stared at her empty plate.

"Dear Lord, forgive us our trespasses," Sam snapped.

Cade looked up, saw his host's face darken, and quickly steepled his hands in prayer. Reluctantly, Maggie did the same.

"And thank you for this bountiful dinner cooked by one of your most priceless gifts to the world, my wonderful daughter-in-law," Sam said with a wink at Emma, "and bless this house and the people seated here at our table. Also bless those who are out on the mountain protecting us from harm. Amen."

"Amen," answered the people around the table.

Everyone started helping themselves to the sumptuous feast before them. Cade put a negligible amount of each dish on his wife's plate, and then without a thought started spoon feeding her.

Emma looked worriedly at Sam. Sam shrugged. So long as Cade seemed happy to care for his disabled wife, there wasn't much to say. Cade may or may not be right about the ranch having a positive effect on Sylvie's disability.

"After dessert," Jenny said innocently. "I'm gonna sing you my song, 'A Donkey Named Mike'."

"Let me guess, it's about your donkey," Cade stated, crinkling up his nose and making a funny face at Jenny.

"You never know, it might be about another donkey named Mike," Jenny teased Cade back.

"Speaking of donkeys," added Cole, "I have someone interested in adopting him."

"About that…," Emma started.

"Oh, no, we can't let Mike go, Patch has already bonded with him," Mary gasped, dropping a full ladle of mashed potatoes on the table.

"Nooooo," Jenny wailed, tearing up.

"Good Heavens, child," Maggie growled. "Ease up on that caterwauling."

"Oh, Geez, I am sorry," Cole stammered, back peddling.

"That's enough, Jenny," Sam scolded his granddaughter. "Dry your tears. Your mother and I have already decided that Mike is a Montana now."

"At least if it is okay with the sheriff," Emma said, turning to Cole.

"No problem here," Cole replied, hands up in the air. "I know when I'm defeated."

Cole grinned.

"You cheeky jerk, you knew they'd keep him all along, didn't you," Dee scolded the sheriff.

"Busted," Cole agreed as he speared a piece of turkey.

"Cole Trane, you devil," Emma wagged a finger at him.

"I was the one who found Mike after the drug dealers rolled the stolen truck they were driving. Mike got thrown out of the truck bed into a muddy ditch. The guys in the truck weren't so lucky," Dee confided.

Jenny pushed away from the table and threw herself at Dee.

"I love you, Dee," Jenny warbled.

"I love you too, kiddo," Dee blushed.

"I can't wait to hear your song," Zoe declared, brandishing her napkin like a bullfighter's cape. She then flashed Sam a toothy smile.

Mary grinned in amusement.

Emma and Dee glanced at each other and burst into a fit of schoolgirl giggles.

Maggie snorted in disgust.

Cole appeared lost, wondering what he had just missed.

Cade winked at Sam for some unknown reason.

Sam hated 'winkers'. Winkers were untrustworthy in Sam's opinion.

"Lord, help me," Sam murmured into his hand, glimpsing hand movement from Sylvie. He glanced down and then sideways so that no one at the table would realize he was looking at the frail woman in the wheelchair to his right.

Sylvie gripped the wheelchair's arms so hard that her knuckles were white. A tiny tear appeared at the corner of one eye. Her mouth quivered. After a moment, her hands and face relaxed.

Well, well, well, Sam thought, amused. Was that a laugh?

Chapter Seven

A horse is worth more than riches.
Spanish Proverb

The Montana family and their new guests sat scattered about the living room on chairs or on the one antique oak claw foot rose adorned couch, all except for Dee Gallant, the sheriff and his deputy who had left for home after dinner, their long day done.

Emma had seen her friend cast a wistful look at Cole before riding away on her bay gelding. Guilt niggled at her heart. Emma had never intentionally led Cole on. Cole was sweet on her, but she was still in love with Cleve. In her heart, she knew that Cleve would want her to move on and learn to love again, but Cleve Montana was a hard act to follow.

She had enjoyed a private chuckle when she noticed her son looking just as longingly at the Ranger as Cole did at her when Dee trotted away into the sunset. Ah, teen crushes. She grinned. She had married her teen crush.

"So I am Jenny Montana and this is my song 'A Donkey Named Mike'," Jenny said breathlessly, looking around the room, her cheeks as rosy as her face, her lilac dress sporting a dime-sized gravy stain on the skirt.

Mary clapped encouragement.

Jenny grinned.

"This should be interesting," Emma heard her father-in-law mumble.

She shook a warning finger at him. He smiled back.

"I'm looking forward to this," Cade cheered from his seat between his invalid wife and Maggie.

Maggie drank her tea, her pinkie raised in the air like a proper society lady.

"Me too, break a leg, Jenny," Zoe chortled.

"I don't plan on breaking any bones, I'm just gonna sing my song, Mrs Puddicombe," Jenny gushed, puzzled by everyone's laughter.

"It's just a theatre saying," Mary giggled.

"It means good luck," Zoe said.

"Oh, okay," Jenny chirped.

"Ready, BJ," she asked her brother.

BJ pulled out a harmonica and blew a note.

"Here we go," Jenny continued, posing so that her chin was lifted, and her hands were together, folded primly in front of her like she was at a church recital.

Emma held her breath, proud of her daughter and slightly fearful for her too. She was only eight, after all.

BJ drew in his breath and blew out a 'C' note. He played a soft toe tapping country beat, and then Jenny began her song:

Well, I'm a donkey named Mike.
Yes, I'm a donkey named Mike.
I'm fifty years-old, or so I am told.
All I know is that I feel old.
California's is the place where I started,
Then my herd, we were captured and parted.
I ended up inside a pen.
And that's where I met, my friend Clem.
Well, I'm a donkey named Mike.
Yes, I'm a donkey named Mike.

Off to the desert, we did go
In search of mountains full of gold.
Then old Clem he struck it rich
And took me home to meet the witch.
She didn't like me, just her hens.
I ended up back inside a pen
Well, I'm a donkey named Mike.
Yes, I'm a donkey named Mike.

I met a woman with flowers in her hair,
Who lived in a place where music filled the air.
I was painted pink and all shades of purple.
Thank goodness, she didn't own a girdle.
Life was good with Persephone.
It was as sweet as honey bees
Well, I'm a donkey named Mike.
Yes, I'm a donkey named Mike.

With tears flowing from her eyes,

She hugged me close and said, "Goodbye".
I was loaded into a van,
And once again was inside a pen.
With a wink and a nod, a man said 'Hello',
And whisked me off to Buffalo.
Well, I'm a donkey named Mike.
Yes, I'm a donkey named Mike.

I walked up a ramp onto a train,
Arrived in town and I was dead lame.
The man he said that wouldn't do,
And shipped me off to turn me into glue.
A nice old lady came to rescue me,
And that's how I ended up in Tennessee.
Well, I'm a donkey named Mike.
Yes, I'm a donkey named Mike.

I live on a farm that's lush and green,
I can run wild and I can live free.
Truth be told, my gait has slowed,
But, what can I say, I'm fifty years-old?
Well, I'm a donkey named Mike.
Yes, I'm a donkey named Mike.
Well, I'm a donkey named Mike.
Yes, I'm a donkey named Mike.

Emma laughed and clapped loudly, jumping to her feet and racing to her daughter to wrap her in her arms. She was so proud of her daughter. Her heart was full to bursting.

Everyone in the room except for Maggie had joined in on the last chorus, stomping their feet and clapping in time with Jenny's song. Sylvie's right foot was involuntarily tapping on the wheelchair's foot rest.

"Splendid job," Mary shouted.

"Marvelous," Zoe agreed.

"You too, BJ," Sam rumbled, nudging his grandson.

"Thanks," BJ blushed.

Jenny grinned and bowed like a superstar.

"You are very talented young lady," Cade encouraged her.

"I thought I'd leave out the part where Mike got stolen by drug smugglers and had his ear cut off," Jenny babbled. "That's just too sad."

"What a wonderful and highly entertaining evening," Zoe said, drawing Jenny in for a hug. "If you don't all mind, I'm going to retreat to my room to read for a while before bed. It has been an eventful day and I'm feeling it."

"And I'm going to pay one last visit to Patch, and his friend, a very famous donkey named Mike," Mary agreed.

"What about you, Mags? Do you want to check on the horses," Cade asked Maggie, "before I get Sylvie settled for the night?"

"It's been such an insufferable day, I'd appreciate a long soak in the bath," Maggie crooned.

"Of course," Emma replied, jumping to her feet, a bit annoyed at herself for wanting to please this irritating woman, but it was her job. "I'll get you some fresh towels. There are lots of bubble bath and bath salts in the upstairs bathroom, so please feel free to use any that's there."

"That won't be necessary," Maggie purred, "I've brought my own towels and bath oils."

"Oh, okay," Emma stammered.

Maggie stood up and with a pointed look at Cade, followed Zoe up the stairs.

Emma glanced helplessly at Sam. He shrugged in return, just as confused.

Cade looked flustered.

"I am sorry," he stuttered, tucking his wife's shawl around her shoulders. "Maggie's well…"

"Maggie is Maggie," Sam offered.

"Something like that," Cade agreed. "She never used to be so dour."

Jenny stood with her arms at her sides, her lower lip quivering, wondering what just happened. Why was everyone suddenly leaving?

Mary saw Jenny's distress and pulled her in close.

"Would you like to come with me out to the barn and help me brush Patch," Mary asked the child. "We'll give Mike a curry down too."

Jenny's eyes brightened.

"Really, you'll let me brush your stallion," Jenny's voice warbled.

"If your granddad says it's okay, I will," Mary glanced up at Sam.

"Go ahead," Sam beamed.

"That was a wonderful ode to a donkey," Cade told Jenny. "It was by far the best donkey song that I've ever heard."

"Thank you, Mr O'Hara," Jenny beamed.

96

"Put your jeans on before heading out to the barn," Emma told her daughter.

"You bet, Mom. Woohoo, I'm going to snuggle with Patch," Jenny shouted as she raced up the stairs two at a time.

"BJ, lets go pick out the stalls and make sure all them studs are bedded down for the night," Sam told his grandson.

"Yes, sir," BJ grinned, tucking his harmonica back in his shirt pocket.

"Ya'll need any help with Sylvie," Emma asked, still not sure how to help or what was expected of her regarding Sylvie's care.

"Actually, Emma, if you can spare some towels and soap, I can tend to my wife's needs," Cade replied graciously, standing up. He wheeled his wife around and pushed her towards the bedroom, whistling Jenny's song as he did so.

Emma smiled.

She liked Cade.

Cade was so devoted to his wife.

Emma wondered who would look after her in her old age. Her father-in-law had her to help him if ever he needed it, but she had nobody but her children. Lord forbid that she ever became a burden to them. And yet, here was Cade, attending to his wife's every need with a smile on his face and a gentleness the like of which she had never seen in a man. Mrs O'Hara was a lucky woman.

Maybe it was time to give Cole a chance… she knew he cared for her… but then the image of Gus Rodriquez flashed through her mind… his dark brown eyes, broad chest, and brawny arms. Oh, Heavens, she had to stop this line of thinking.

Emma felt eyes upon her. She looked up and saw her father-in-law looking at her oddly. His eyes were narrow and his moustache was quivering.

"What," she blurted out, a little too harshly. It would be just like Sam to read her mind.

"Nothing," Sam chortled. "Come on BJ, let's go finish our chores."

Sam continued to laugh lightly as he walked by, one hand on his grandson's shoulder.

Emma's cheeks burned. She felt as if she was going to burst into flames. It was if she was being roasted over the Devil's own fire pit. She grabbed a Reader's Digest magazine off the table and began fanning herself, her thoughts drifting back to Gus Rodriquez. Thankfully, she was the only one left in the living room to see her loss of composure.

Sam sat in his favourite chair, a leather lazy boy the color of charred wood, with his feet up, reading the latest issue of *Western Horseman* beneath a small table lamp. Hank Williams 'Honky Tonk Blues' played softly on the radio on the end table beside him. He downed a shot glass full of Johnny Walker; his painkiller of choice.

He had moved his bed into the library room and study two years earlier, happy not to be climbing up and down the stairs at all hours of the night during calving season. Arthritis was a bitch. He poured himself another shot.

His bedroom was cozy. Books about horses, cattle, veterinary techniques, tattered Louis L'Amour and Zane Grey westerns lay jumbled together, along with many worn editions of horsemanship and cattlemen's magazines. They filled every nook and crevasse.

His boots were tucked beneath the table beside him. Emma was in bed, and so was everyone else, so why leave his boots at the door when he wanted to do one more late-night feed, anyway.

He took a sip of whiskey. It burned his throat pleasantly, the pungent smell reminding him of old friends, campfires, and his dear sweet Adelaide.

Outside, a night owl hooted. Crickets chirped. A low mist had drifted in at sunset, covering the valley in a tepid fog. A half moon hung low in the star-spangled sky.

He didn't envy the deputies and ATF men sleeping, backs against hard stone, out on the mountain, hoping to glimpse a fire, or hear a muffled curse, allowing them to close in on the notorious Tommy Cortez. It was a job for much younger men than he, hard of body and resilient.

That was the primary reason for his sleeplessness. Tommy Cortez could be anywhere, up the mountain or hiding in the valley waiting for dark to steal a truck or a horse. Sam didn't know much about him, only that the fugitive was dangerous.

Sam had vetoed Cole coming back to stay the night. He and Emma had enough on their plate with all these newcomers.

Sam downed his drink.

He thought he heard a creaking of a stair.

He listened. A chorus of frogs joined the crickets. That was it.

Sam swore he heard the front door open.

He opened his bedroom door and padded out into the darkened living room. A night light illuminated the kitchen off to the side. There was no one there.

He glanced up the stairs. Emma had left the upstairs hall light on so that the ladies could find their way to the bathroom if needed. There was no movement upstairs either.

Sam sighed and returned to his room. A faint light shone beneath the crack under the O'Hara's closed bedroom door. All seemed quiet in their room.

Sam tugged his boots back on. May as well check on the horses, he thought. There would be no sleep tonight, not until Cortez was apprehended at any rate.

Sam picked up the shotgun propped against the wall beside the front door.

He stepped out into the night.

The air was fresh. The smell of fresh cut hay filled the air with its grassy, pungent odour. He should cut his own now, too. Maybe he'd call Anson Williams in the morning to see if his son was available to help them this year. It was too much to expect BJ to handle the fields too.

It was too bad really, as they were having an excellent year. They'd get three cuts this year.

There was a ghostly flash of white in the shadows inside the barn. Sam's heart quickened, the hair rising on the back of his neck.

A horse nickered softly.

One horse thumped a leg against the stall door.

Sam raised the gun, thumbed back the trigger, and crept stealthily across the yard, making sure he kept to the shadows himself.

Might be Cortez, he thought. Well, good luck to him if he thinks he's going to get away on one of those stallions!

Sam inched his way forward, taking care to be quieter than a fox in a chicken pen.

He slipped by Mary's truck and trailer, bending over to make himself a smaller target. Ominous shadows provided excellent cover between the trailers.

He lifted the gun and flicked on the barn's main light.

"Bernie, why haven't you changed Zippo's rug," Zoe murmured. She stood inside her stallion's stall wearing nothing but a white lace nightgown. Her feet were bare. She leaned over and unbuckled the nutmeg coloured rug's belly bands. "His blue padded rug is his night rug, honey, I keep telling you that."

"Mrs Puddicombe," Sam asked, letting the trigger down gently on the shotgun.

"Oh, sweetheart, I know," Zoe prattled on. "Zippo is getting old, just like me. He does love his soft cushy rugs though, don't you, boy."

"Mrs Puddicombe… Zoe," Sam breathed, propping the shotgun against the wall outside of the stall, and then slipping inside.

The regal Andalusian stallion lowered his head and snuffled Sam's hand. He then nosed his owner, his breath hot against her face. The stud looked from Zoe to Sam and then back again with quick, intelligent eyes.

The stallion's gentleness amazed Sam, given his leaps and escapades the previous day. He wondered if the stud was used to these midnight visits. The thought chilled Sam to the bone.

Sam placed a hand on either side of Zoe's shoulders. She leaned back into Sam's chest and sighed heavily.

"What are we going to do about Esperanza," Zoe groaned. "I can't bear to lose her, Andre."

"Esperanza will be fine," Sam whispered to the distraught woman. He supposed that Esperanza may have been the filly's mother.

"Are you sure," Zoe wept. "Maybe the vet is wrong. Maybe she will get better."

"I'm sure she will," Sam crooned, slowly leading the woman to the door. He let her go for a moment to re-fasten the belly bands on the stallion's rug, and then quickly returned to her side.

"Promise," she squeaked.

"Promise," Sam murmured, gently wrapping one arm around her shoulder while he closed the door behind them. The stud looked on. Sam could have sworn the horse had just nodded at him in approval.

He slipped the stall door's bolt into place.

So long as Sam could get Zoe safely into bed, he was willing to pretend to be any one of the woman's deceased husbands.

"Okay," she murmured.

Sam tucked the shotgun under one arm and escorted the puzzled woman back to the house. He would have to talk to Emma in the morning about what to do about Zoe's midnight wanderings. Heaven forbid that she wandered out into the pastures and got lost.

He now knew why Zoe Puddicombe had come to stay at *The Silver Spurs Home for Aging Cowgirls.* His heart went out to her.

He had no intention of becoming husband number seven, but she was a good woman and he vowed not to let anything happen to Zoe while she lived under his roof.

Chapter Eight

Good people get cheated, just as good horses get ridden.
Chinese Proverb

Sam pushed the door open to Zoe's room. It squeaked like a baby mouse. He made a mental note to oil the hinges in the morning.

"Jerry be a dear and make me a hot cocoa," Zoe said as Sam guided her into her bedroom.

"I can do that," Sam replied huskily, his heart close to breaking for the capable horse woman he was only beginning to get to know.

"What's going on? It's after midnight," Emma asked, her sleepy-eyed form appearing in silhouette against the doorway.

Sam guided Zoe to the bed. She sat down and let out a long dragged out sigh. Her bare feet were dirt covered. Cedar shavings and tiny pebbles dotted the floor.

"Mrs Puddicombe is a tad confused," Sam whispered. "Grab a facecloth and towel for me, will you?"

"Yeah, okay," Emma answered, her eyes rimmed with sleep crust.

"Poor Esperanza, she hurts so," Zoe wept quietly. "What shall I do?"

"Don't worry, the vet is looking after her," Sam crooned, not sure of what else to say. Obviously, the horse had not been okay.

Emma returned with a hot washcloth and a towel. All hints of sleepiness fell from her when she saw the horse box shavings on Zoe's feet and tangled in the bottom of her nightgown.

Emma bent down to wash the dirt and shavings off her charge's bare feet and pulled a few stray strands of hay out of Zoe's cotton shift.

"What happened?"

"Zoe took a midnight trip to the barn to visit Zippo."

"You're kidding," she gasped.

"Mom, what's going on," a sleepy faced Jenny asked, appearing at the door way.

"Mrs Puddicombe had a brief adventure," Sam whispered to his granddaughter.

"Is she okay," the adolescent girl cried worriedly.

"She's fine, honey, go back to bed," Emma assured her.

"Is that Samantha, Walter," Zoe mumbled, falling back onto the bed. "Tell her not to bother me. I don't want to argue anymore."

Emma and Sam exchanged a worried glance.

"W'as up," BJ rumbled, also appearing in the doorway.

"I'll tuck Mrs Puddicombe in, you deal with the kids," Sam advised his daughter-in-law.

Emma finished cleaning up and tucked the facecloth and towel under her arm.

"Come on, kids, back to bed," Emma commanded, rounding up her children and scooting them back into their bedroom, which was beside Zoe's.

"Zoe will be all right, won't she," Jenny queried her mother.

"Zoe's fine, she's over tired," Emma said.

"I don't mind helping if you need it," BJ whispered. "I like Mrs Puddicombe. She can really sit on a horse."

"You're just like your grandfather," Emma chortled. "Leave it to you to mention a woman's horsemanship skills in the middle of the night."

"What's wrong with that," BJ muttered, rubbing the sleep from his eyes.

"Nothing. Nothing at all," his mother grinned.

Sam listened to Emma settle the children back down as he gently lifted Zoe's feet and tucked them under the covers. She immediately rolled over and snored softly.

He wondered if Zoe had the start of dementia. Maybe she had simply been sleepwalking? Either way, he would ask Emma to have a chat with her in the morning.

With a backwards glance at the sleeping woman, he closed the bedroom door and prayed that the rest of the night would be a quiet one. At least none of their other tenants had been disturbed.

Emma walked back into the hall and closed the door to the children's bedroom softly behind her.

"You go back to bed," Sam advised her. "I'll be up for a while yet. I want to do a walk through the barn again and check on all the horses."

"Are you sure? I can help if you want?"

"You're dead on your feet. Go back to bed," Sam insisted.

Sam tenderly kissed the top of Emma's head. She smiled wearily and headed back to her own bedroom.

Sam stood in the hall for a few minutes, not wanting to leave until he knew that all was quiet.

Satisfied that everyone in the house was asleep, he crept down the stairs and headed back out to the barn, shotgun in hand.

Jenny lay in the bottom bunk bed, her eyes wide open. The southwest breeze brushed its warm breath against her face as she turned to look out the window.

The half moon glowed softly in the sky, rising to its full lunar height. It speckled the room with silvery shadows. The leaves on the lone oak tree outside rustled in the night breeze; one branch tip-tapping against the window.

The night was alive with insects and reptiles. Their chorus was both soothing and annoying as it kept her awake.

Jenny thought she heard Rosie whinny, but it may have been one of the other ranch horses.

BJ's breathing changed from low to high as he turned over in bed, causing the bed springs to squawk.

The door across the hall squeaked open. The light beneath the door to her room grew brighter. The door closed gently, and the light went out. Heavy footsteps thumped along the old wooden planks of the hallway.

Jenny threw back the covers and slunk across the room. She opened the door a crack and peeked out. She gasped, her eyes widening in alarm.

"Shhh, it's okay," Cade whispered to Jenny.

"What are you doing here," she cried. "Your room is downstairs."

"I was checking on Maggie," he crooned. "I wanted to make sure she was okay."

"No, you weren't," Jenny stated. "It's the middle of the night."

"Don't argue with me, little one," Cade threatened mildly. "Good girls aren't up in the middle of the night either."

"I'm gonna go get my grandpa," Jenny seethed, not liking this one iota. Even if Mr O'Hara was a friend of Miss Carroll's, he shouldn't be creeping into her room late at night.

"No, don't do that," Cade wheedled.

"Yeah, I am," she said, trying to barge past him.

Cade grabbed her by the arm and whipped her around.

Jenny was about to scream for her mother when the angry man said: "How about I give you two bucks and we'll forget all about this."

Jenny shut her mouth, stifling her retort. She thought for a moment.

"Ten bucks."

"You drive a hard bargain," Cade grumbled, relieved.

"Pay up then," Jenny quipped, holding out one hand.

"I'm in my pajamas," the old man snorted. "Rain check?"

"In the morning or I tell Grandpa."

"What's going on," BJ whispered behind her.

"Nothing," Jenny replied innocently.

Cade put his finger to his lips and continued to sneak down the stairs, Jenny watching him go. He turned left at the bottom of the stairs, heading for his bedroom.

Jenny returned to her bedroom, shutting the door behind her.

"What was all that about," BJ mumbled grumpily.

"Nothing, you're dreaming," she told her brother as she climbed back into the lower bunk bed.

"That wasn't nothing," her brother growled.

"I'll tell you in the morning," she replied, "maybe."

BJ harrumphed and went back to sleep.

Jenny grinned and thought about what to do with ten dollars.

Sam ambled out onto the porch, a coffee cup in one hand, the shotgun held lightly and with ease in the other. What a night, he thought.

He was glad that Emma had brewed a fresh pot of coffee in the thermos pot that she and the grandkids had given him for Christmas six years ago. They still owned three hundred cattle then. The coffee thermos had been a godsend during calving season. It had also come in handy when Checkers was born. Penny had laboured long and hard throughout the night before giving birth to the fancy colt.

Sam turned right when he entered the barn, flipped on the tack room light, and propped the shotgun against the tack room door.

The barn smelled of cedar shavings, horse sweat, manure and hay. It was an intoxicating mix for old cowboys like him.

He sauntered down the aisle, stopping to give the grey Andalusian stallion a scratch on the forehead. He looked into Zoe's filly's stall and she pinned back her ears.

"Stop, you're scaring me," he joked.

"She terrifies me," a masculine voice echoed from farther inside the barn.

"You were sleeping so peacefully on that hay bale, I didn't want to wake you," Sam jested.

Gus chuckled.

The ATF lieutenant sat up, the back of his bullet-proof vest and pants covered in hay. He pushed himself off the hay bale he had been resting on and retrieved his Sharps rifle, carefully rubbing the sleep from his eyes. He tucked his helmet under one arm.

"Just couldn't stay away, huh," Sam said.

"I was worried Cortez would double back and head down here to the ranch since you're the closest spread. My men are hunkered down at the base of the mountain."

"Hmmm," Sam mumbled. "That was a long walk."

"It was. That coffee smells wonderful," Gus said, slipping the rifle's strap over his shoulder.

"There's more at the house if you want some," Sam said.

"I'll take you up on that."

Sam walked the lieutenant up to the house.

"The sheriff's not here," he fumed, glancing first into the living room and then into the kitchen as they entered the ranch house.

"Naw, I told him to 'get' after dinner and to take his deputy with him. I got it covered," Sam growled, lifting the shotgun.

Gus chortled.

Sam motioned for the lieutenant to help himself. The lieutenant obliged and fixed himself a cup of coffee with double cream and sugar.

"I still got to do night feed," Sam continued. "You can settle down on the couch or back on that hay bale in the barn, whichever you feel is more comfortable."

Gus grinned and nodded towards the couch.

"That's what I expected," Sam chortled.

"Want some help with the horses?"

"Nope," Sam said, topping up his coffee mug. The horses didn't really need another night feed, but it made Sam feel better to keep watch over them.

Gus took his coffee into the living room. He kicked off his boots but didn't remove his bullet-proof vest. He slipped his handgun out of its holster, checked the safety, and placed it on the coffee table within easy reach. He lowered the rifle to the floor, once again keeping it a mere hand's breadth away.

"Don't be scaring Emma or my grandkids in the morning," Sam advised him, "or I might have to shoot you myself."

"What about all the other folks you got living here," Gus snorted, his eyes instantly closing as he laid his head down on a throw pillow.

"Them either," Sam grinned before heading out the door.

Chapter Nine

A pony is a childhood dream. A horse is an adulthood treasure.
Rebecca Carroll

Emma crawled down the stairs, exhausted from worrying about Zoe and Zoe's midnight rambling. She wore a ragged white terry-cloth robe, the one that she and Cleve had pinched from their honeymoon suite at Disney World, fastened with a bright pink fuzzy belt. Florescent pink fuzzy slippers completed the ensemble. Some might have chosen Niagara Falls, the Bahamas or Hawaii for their honeymoon, but Cleve and Emma had wanted to have fun before Cleve's first deployment.

A black-haired male head popped up over top of the couch in the living room.

"Good morning, Emma," the amused voice echoed through the living room.

Emma shrieked!

"Oh, oh," Gus chuckled.

"So much for not scaring my daughter-in-law," a red-eyed Sam declared from the doorway to his bedroom. He still wore the clothes from the day before.

"Is everything all right," Cade called, throwing open the door to his bedroom. He tied up the corners of his night robe as he raced into the living room.

"Who screamed? Is the gun smuggler in the house," hollered Mary from the top of the stairs.

"Mom, are you okay," a terrified Jenny wailed from behind Mary, once again her face as scarlet as her hair.

"Where's the banshee," Zoey joked, resting a comforting hand on Jenny's slim shoulders.

"Good heavens, what is all that racket? It's ungodly early," Maggie grumbled, pushing past the three at the top of the stairs to cast a baleful glance Emma's way.

"Sorry everyone," Emma flushed with embarrassment. "I'm not used to armour clad men popping their heads up over my couch."

"My bad," Gus waved to the ladies.

Mary and Zoe grinned.

"Oooh, I'd like to wake up to that," Zoe whispered in Mary's ear.

"Can't say I'd mind either," she muttered.

"Go back to bed everyone, it's only seven," Emma said, still flustered. "Breakfast won't be for another hour and a half."

"Can I make you coffee, Em" Gus asked, standing up. He had unfastened his vest during the night. His khaki coloured shirt stood partially unbuttoned, revealing a bronzed muscled chest beneath it.

"Yummy," Zoey crooned.

"Indubitably," Mary joked.

Maggie huffed and spun on her heels, her open-toed slippers causing her to slip and almost topple into the wall. It seemed even Maggie wasn't immune to the gorgeous ATF agent's charms.

"God, Maggie, I hate you already," Zoey hissed at the departing woman's back.

"You don't even know me," the angry woman growled, spinning around.

"It's because even startled awake by a woman's terrified cry, you look marvellous," Mary chuckled.

For the first time since arriving at the ranch, Maggie Carroll smiled. Her face brightened, the lines around her mouth and on her forehead softening. She chuckled lightly.

Maggie ran a hand through her hair and then sauntered back to her room with a Marilyn Monroe walk.

The ladies burst out laughing.

Maggie waved an adoring hand over her head.

At the bottom of the stairs, Emma entreated Gus, "Coffee would be nice. It's not often someone makes it for me."

"Go back to bed, Sam," Gus rumbled, casting a delighted look towards Emma's bleary eyed father-in-law. "I got this."

Sam grumbled incoherently and went back to his bedroom, slamming his door shut, not at all amused.

Cade chuckled.

"Now that I know our fair lady is safe, I think I'll return to bed too for a short kip before breakfast," the illustrious Cade said with a dandy's bow.

Emma smiled and turned towards the kitchen.

"Wait a minute, where is BJ," she asked, preparing to race up the stairs.

"He's already gone," Gus replied, buttoning up his shirt as he walked towards Emma. "Those horses are sure spoiled. Heavens, midnight snacks and breakfast at the crack of dawn, I should be so lucky."

Emma chuckled.

"Come on, I'll fix us some toast while you make the coffee," she sighed. "What are you doing here, anyway?"

"I hiked in late last night. My men have everything under control, and I wanted to make sure you were all right."

"Except for the white hairs you just gave me, I'm fine, Emma joked.

"Sorry."

Emma put some toast in the toaster while Gus made the coffee, both disturbed and titillated by the closeness of the former Marine's body next to hers.

"Sam tells me that expensive rig out there belongs to your three new tenants," he queried, moving closer. "I am assuming I just met two. Where's the third?"

"In bed. She's an invalid. That was her husband, Cade, you just met."

Emma drank in the scent of the mountain wildflowers, cedar, and man musk that drifted off the former marine. There was also the faintest whiff of horse. Her hands trembled as she reached for two side plates from the cupboard.

The toast popped up, startling Emma once again.

Gus grinned as he reached around her for two fresh coffee mugs.

Emma's heart quickened.

"The O'Hara's and their friend, Maggie Carroll, arrived late yesterday afternoon," she said, annoyed by the tremble in her voice and her need to fill the space between them with idle chitchat.

She felt Gus' fingers brush against her neck. He lifted the hair from her face and turned her around.

Emma's pulse raced. Her breath caught in her throat.

"Gus, I...," she said breathlessly.

He looked deep into her blue eyes.

Emma shivered.

They heard the roll of gravel beneath tires as the sheriff drove into the yard.

Gus sighed and let Emma's hair fall back into place.

Emma's wasn't ready for this. Gus was handsome, strong, and devoted to her and the kids, but he had breezed back into her life in a hail of drama and jeopardy. She hadn't talked to him or had a letter from him in almost three years. Did he have a girlfriend? Was he married? Engaged? What were his long-term intentions?

Damn, she thought, I'm in over my head in less than fifteen minutes. Ugh!

Emma heard Cole shout a 'hello' to BJ in the barn and then the stomp of boots on the front porch. He knocked politely before entering.

Cole's face paled when he walked into the kitchen. He hitched up his gun belt, and glowered at Gus hovering over the coffee pot beside his lady.

"Morning, Lieutenant," Cole snapped.

"Sheriff," Gus nodded a greeting.

"You're early this morning, Cole," Emma said with forced bravado. "Coffee won't be ready for another few minutes."

"S'okay, I brought my own," the sheriff muttered, lifting a traveller's mug. "I wanted to make sure Sam had no problems during the night."

"Only one," Sam grumbled, walking into the kitchen, his hair wet from the shower. He wore a clean cotton plaid shirt and blue jeans.

"I see that," Cole replied stiffly.

"I wasn't talking about the lieutenant," Sam replied.

"One of our guests took a midnight stroll," Emma shrugged sheepishly.

"Not the best time to be doing that," Gus exclaimed.

"No time is the best time for doing that," Sam snorted, taking a seat at the table.

"Early onset dementia," Cole said knowingly. "My aunt is dealing with that too."

Gus looked puzzled.

"You didn't read the sign coming in," Cole quipped.

Gus' face was blank.

"*The Silver Spurs Home for Aging Cowgirls* is open for business," Sam declared.

"Oh," Gus mumbled, raising an eyebrow. "I thought I saw you leading a lady back to the house when I was arriving. Wasn't sure I should ask about it."

"What you do is you get a push button lock for the door," Cole replied sagely, ignoring Gus' comments, "and you reverse the handle so that the door locks with a key from the inside instead of the outside. That way you can lock the door at night so you don't have to worry about your residents wandering. If you have an emergency, the ambulance or firefighters, or me, can open up the door from the outside. That's what auntie did. Worked like a charm."

"That makes sense," Sam nodded. "I'll drive into town today and go and fetch one."

"It's an inexpensive solution," Gus grinned. "Nice."

"Anyway, like I just said to Cole, Sam, coffee won't be ready for a few minutes."

"I can wait," Sam said, taking a seat at the table.

"Me too," Cole replied, doing the same.

"The testosterone level in this room just went up a notch," Sam chortled, taking the two suitors measure. "Feels like I'm caught between two bulls during mating season."

Emma glared at her father-in-law. He was no help at all. The wide grin on his face attested to that.

"You both going to stay for breakfast," she asked the crime fighting duo.

"Yes, ma'am," Gus said authoritatively.

"If you don't mind," Cole responded politely.

"I don't mind at all, Sheriff," Emma replied with a calmness she didn't really feel. "I think I'll go get dressed first though."

"That's a fine idea," Sam chortled, glancing down at Emma's large fuzzy pink slippers. "Maybe put some shoes on while you're at it."

Emma playfully swatted her father-in-law on the arm as she walked by.

All three of the men laughed at her.

Emma decided that she'd make the men a quick breakfast and get them out the door before the rest of the household barnstormed the kitchen.

Breakfast was quick and simple: scrambled eggs, bacon and toast. The men bulldozed their way through a dozen eggs and a pound of bacon in record time. Emma scooted them out the door and began cooking for the next round of people to flood the kitchen.

Cade wheeled in his wife, a smile on his face, Sylvie sitting mute in her chair as always. It tore a hole in Emma's heart thinking of the dependent world that Cade's wife lived in. It hurt to think how trapped that active mind was inside a body that wouldn't respond. She knew Sylvie caught what was going on around her by the look on her face and the flash in her eyes when Sylvie thought no one was watching.

Zoe brushed by Cade, casually flipping her brightly coloured neck scarf in his face as she sashayed by him.

Cade laughed, his grey eyes lighting up.

Obviously, Zoe's midnight ramble hadn't affected her high spirit.

"Good morning, Miss Zoe," Cade purred.

"Good morning, Mr Cade," she teased, batting her eyelids at him.

Cade chuckled and pushed his wife's wheelchair up to the table.

Maggie elbowed Cade none too gently as she slipped into the seat beside Cade.

Mary and Jenny skipped into the room holding hands and singing the chorus to *A Donkey named Mike*.

"Well, I'm a donkey named Mike," the two sang. "Yes, I'm a donkey named Mike."

Emma laughed. It seemed her daughter's wish had come true: she had at least one cowboy grandma. The rest of the ladies weren't exactly grandma material.

"Where's that hunk of a father-in-law of yours this morning," Zoe quizzed her.

Mary bowed to Jenny as Jenny pulled out a chair for her. Mary smiled coyly and then sat down with a flourish. Jenny giggled.

"He's gone out to the barn to fetch BJ," Emma chuckled.

"Actually, at the moment, it looks like he's telling those two handsome men off," Maggie beamed.

That woman was so annoying, Emma seethed.

"Oh," Emma said, glancing out the kitchen window.

Sam stood in the yard wagging a warning finger at the two men straddling the sheriff's three wheeled trike. Cole drove and Gus sat grim faced behind him, his rifle on his back, his helmet shading his eyes.

"I wonder what that's all about," Cade remarked casually.

"I expect Sam is telling them we don't need a deputy around all day getting under foot," Emma lied, knowing instinctively that her father-in-law was warning them not to hurt her. Sam was over-protective of his family. Her stomach flip-flopped. Who'd have thought, two men vying for her hand. She smoothed down her apron. "Now, who wants eggs, who wants pancakes, and who wants both?"

"Both, please," Jenny and Mary said together. The pair burst into yet another fit of giggles.

"Do you have any fruit and granola," Maggie asked.

"I guess I can whip something up," Emma replied.

"You don't whip up granola, dear, it whips you," Maggie chortled, thinking her comment smart.

Emma didn't get it.

Cade noticed Emma's confusion and came to the rescue.

"You don't have to cook the granola. Maggie likes everything raw - fruit, granola…"

"Men," Zoe added smoothly.

Cade roared with laughter. His wife's eyebrow twitched. Maggie smirked.

Jenny raced around the table and whispered something into Cade's ear. He nodded and grinned.

"Jenny, there are no secrets in this household," Emma scolded her daughter.

Cade and Jenny high-fived each other.

"Sorry, Mom won't happen again," the little girl cried as she raced back around the table and slid into her seat beside Mary.

Outside, an ATV roared as it sped out of the yard. Moments later, BJ entered the house, kicking his boots off at the door and hanging his straw cowboy hat on a peg by the window.

"Hey, Mom," the boy said. "That smells delicious. I'm so hungry I could eat a horse."

"Not one of mine, I hope," Zoe joked.

"No, ma'am, I like your horses," BJ grinned.

"I'm devastated," Mary quipped, placing a hand over her heart.

"I didn't mean that Mrs Adams."

"Please call me Mary, BJ. Mrs Adams makes me feel so old."

"Yes, ma'am," BJ agreed.

"I'd like a pancake with my eggs too, if you don't mind, Emma," Cade mumbled, fixing himself a cup of coffee and his wife a cup of tea.

"What about Sylvie," Emma asked, depositing a plate of pancakes in front of Jenny and a plate of eggs, pancakes and bacon in front of Mary.

"Sylvie eats lighter too. Fruit and granola, if you have some, would be fine; otherwise, just a piece of toast and a scrambled egg."

Emma nodded and took down a box of Quaker's Three-minute oats. She poured some in a bowl and handed it to Maggie.

"What's this," Maggie asked.

"Granola," Emma said. The woman wanted it raw and raw it was.

"Mom, granola and quick oats aren't the same thing," Jenny informed her mother.

"They aren't?"

"No, they aren't," Maggie snorted derisively.

"Hey, I didn't know either until a teacher at school explained the difference to me," Jenny scolded the dark-haired woman across the table.

Emma blushed, embarrassed, and removed the bowl of oats from in front of her 'guest'. She doubted Maggie Carroll would ever become a full-time resident there.

"No matter, Emma, eggs and toast for my two ladies then," Cade replied, smoothing over the ruffled feathers at the table.

"Mrs Puddicombe, er, Zoe, do you think you could give me a riding lesson on Bucky today," BJ piped up, coming to his mother's rescue. "I really want to learn to make Bucky dance like Zippo does."

"What I was doing yesterday is called a Piaffe, BJ," Zoe said, buttering a piece of toast.

"Oh, you're a dressage rider," Maggie asked.

"I'm a Grand Prix rider," Zoe replied with a slight tilt of her head as if schooling a child. "I ride Prix St. George. Zippo and Extravaganza were certified at the FEI World Equestrian Games, and I have competed in the Alltech FEI World Equestrian Games several times with my late husband."

"My, that's a feat," Cade blurted through a mouthful of pancake.

"Both Sylvie and I have competed all over the world," Maggie bragged. "We started in jumpers and competed in the World Games in our day but switched to hunters after a couple of serious falls. Sylvie was the worst. She was always breaking something."

"That's not true," Cade jumped in.

"Of course, it is," Maggie quipped.

Emma deposited an apple, orange, and a banana in front of Maggie, and an empty bowl and a paring knife.

God forgive me, Emma prayed, but this woman was insufferable, and she would not cut up her fruit for her, just out of principle.

"If you really want to learn to ride dressage, BJ, I'll let you ride Zippo," Zoe continued. "I am sure Bucky is an exceptional ranch horse, but he isn't built for dressage."

"Really, you'll let me ride your stallion," BJ beamed, his eyes widening with both shock and delight.

"Awwww," Jenny sulked.

"Are you sure it's safe," Emma queried, worried for her son.

"Zippo is an old campaigner. BJ will be quite safe. Zippo is forgiving in his own way, but there will be no 'cowboying him' as the saying goes."

"That's a bitter fuse to light," Mary drawled. "Cowboys treat their horses with the utmost respect. Their mounts are working horses. They depend on them."

"All the same, Mary, that paint of yours is handsome, but Zippo is like a Picasso painting, he is priceless. He is adept at pirouettes in a piaffe, a half pass in passage and can perform a double canter pirouette."

"I don't understand what that is, but I want to learn it," BJ said.

"Well, then you better eat a hearty breakfast," Emma said, adding another two pancakes to her son's plate.

"I'm looking forward to this too," Cade said. "Do you mind if Sylvie and I watch from the sidelines?"

Zoe smiled lasciviously at Cade.

Maggie simmered.

Sam watched his beaming grandson lead the tall elegant white stallion into the ring. Sam was so proud of him and so glad he was still alive to see it. After Adelaide died, he had almost given up, until his son married Emma and his BJ was born nine months later.

BJ was a terrific kid, steady, and hard working. He seldom complained, no matter how difficult the task. Even with school and what seemed an endless amount of homework, he still found time to help with the cattle. Thanks to that darned donkey and the indubitable Zoe Puddicombe and her Andalusian horses, his grandson smiled a lot more too.

The only thing that worried him was Extravaganza. When Zoe saddled up her filly, Sam had thought she was crazy for taking that temperamental young mare into the ring with the stallion. He trusted the stallion, but the filly was another matter. She was as uppity as Maggie's chestnut stallion. Extravaganza should have been named Tempest, in his opinion.

Zoe laughed, breaking Sam's reverie. It was a high-pitched giggle that was both annoying and charming at the same time. She patted him maternally on the arm and batted her eyelashes as she sashayed by.

Sam had already brought some plastic chairs out of the barn and lined them up in front of the riding ring so that Emma, Mary, Maggie and Cade could watch through the split fence rails. He and Jenny sat on top of the rails. Cade pulled Sylvie's wheelchair up next to him.

Sam swore he saw Sylvie lean forward, transfixed, as Zoe rode the prancing filly around the ring on a relaxed rein.

"Before you mount Zippo, BJ, I want you to stand him perpendicular to the fence," Zoe commanded softly.

Sam thought Zoe looked regal in her black riding breaches, black felt hat, and white blouse. The filly's saddle was black leather, as was the training bridle that Zoe had fitted her with. Her saddle pad was a deep burgundy, the colour of an excellent port. The filly was groomed to perfection, her silver mane and tail glistening. There wasn't a speck of dust on her coat.

Being that Mrs Puddicombe was such a flirt, Sam didn't know if the show was for him or if Zoe always dressed that way. Either way, he had to admit that he was enjoying himself.

Jenny squirmed on the fence beside him.

"Stop it young lady," Sam scolded his granddaughter. "This is a serious riding lesson. You'd do well to clean out the ear wax and listen up."

"Yes, Grandpa," she mumbled.

"Now I want you to place your hand on his shoulder and push gently," Zoe continued.

BJ did as he was told, and the stallion stepped lightly to the left.

"Now square him up and again and put some light pressure on the hind quarters."

Again, BJ did as commanded, placing his hand on the stallion's left hip. The stallion instantly moved his hindquarters to the left.

127

"He's really light to the touch," BJ murmured.

"I want you to remember that once you are up in the saddle, he will respond to every one of your queues. If you are riding a straight line and you look right, your left hip will automatically lift out of the saddle ever so subtly and your right foot will dip down at the heel putting pressure in the stirrup. Zippo will respond to that and move his body away from the pressure. Do you understand?"

"Yes ma'am."

The lesson continued with Zoe quietly spelling out instructions and BJ responding. Before long, Zoe and BJ were riding side-by-side, the grey filly and the white stallion in perfect harmony, step for step. It was a spectacular sight.

"BJ, you look real handsome up there," Emma said, her eyes wide with wonder.

"He does at that," Mary remarked.

"Wait until the girls see him," Cade joked. "He'll be beating them off with a stick."

"Don't be vulgar, Cade," Maggie chided him.

"The girls already have their sights set on him, Cade," Emma laughed. "It starts every year after the first weekend in September."

"I must say, Mrs Puddicombe," Maggie drawled, "that is a remarkable display of horsemanship. Bravo."

Everyone turned to stare at Maggie, shocked into silence. You could have heard the proverbial pin drop.

"Thank you, Ms Carroll," Zoe replied as she and BJ trotted by, not missing a beat.

"Yes, bravo, bravo," Cade said, clapping wildly.

Maggie cast imaginary daggers at Zoe's most enthusiastic of fans.

Zoe called it quits after an hour. The two horses were soaked with sweat. BJ was dripping. Zoe looked as fresh as a daisy.

"Miss Zoe, will you teach me to ride like that when I'm bigger," Jenny asked innocently.

"I would be happy to," Zoe replied, walking her tired filly in a wide circle around the ring to cool off.

"Here that? I'm gonna ride all pretty like that one day, Grandpa," Jenny gushed.

"Well, you know what they say, Jenny-penny," Sam replied with a grin. "A pony is a childhood dream. A horse is an adulthood treasure."

"I'm gonna start praying every night for a horse like Zippo when I grow up."

The feisty, short haired snip of a woman atop the grey filly continued to amaze him. Whatever her issues were whether sleep walking or dementia, Sam vowed that Zoe Puddicombe would always be welcome at the Montana ranch.

Chapter Ten

It is the difficult horses that have the most to give you.
Lendon Gray

Jenny leaned against the stall door, watching BJ brush down Zoe's stallion. The Andalusian was tied to a ring close to the corner feed bucket in his stall, which was unnecessary in Jenny's opinion given that his attention was focused on what was in the bucket.

Jenny reached out to pet him.

"Don't do that, Jen," BJ warned her. "He's protective of his feed bucket. He'll sink his teeth into you."

"No, he won't," Jenny harrumphed.

"Yes, he will," BJ replied crossly. "Mom and Grandpa would be furious if you got bitten and needed to go to the hospital to get stitches."

Jenny's sulk only lasted for a moment. She pulled a ten-dollar bill from her pocket. Cade had sneaked it to her at the breakfast table. She snapped it crisply between both hands.

"What's that," BJ asked, taking a break from combing out the horse's luxurious white mane.

"I got ten bucks," she said, defiantly lifting her chin into the air.

"How'd you get that," BJ asked suspiciously.

"Earned it," she crooned.

"Did not."

"Did."

"Doing what," BJ asked dubiously.

"If you must know I caught Mr O'Hara sneaking out of Miss Carroll's room last night after Grandpa put Mrs Puddicombe back to bed."

"You what," BJ exclaimed. "Jenny, this is serious. Mom and Grandpa will be furious when they hear that. Mr O'Hara is married."

"I don't care. I made ten bucks out of the deal. I'm not gonna tell them and neither are you," Jenny fumed, glaring at her brother.

"Sis, you're gonna go to Hell for that."

BJ tried to snatch the ten-dollar bill from his sister's hand, but she whisked it away and tucked it back inside her jeans.

"Devil's got better things to do than chase after me for ten dollars," Jenny smirked and danced away.

"You need to tell Mom or Grandpa. If you don't, then I will."

"And I'll tell them you're a liar," she yelled and ran from the barn.

The stallion knocked the curry comb flying out of BJ's hand.

"Not you too," he cried, exasperated.

Sam, Cade and BJ had spent the afternoon after BJ's riding lesson building a wheelchair ramp off the side of the front porch. It had proven more difficult than he expected, but most of that was because of Cade.

Sam sighed with gratitude, and finally put his feet up. The clock in the living room chimed eight times. Between the late-night last night and the hectic day, he was plumb worn out.

The TV was blaring in the living room. It was some crazy game show that Cade said he and his wife loved. Sam didn't understand the appeal and was happy to retire to his bedroom and pour himself a drink.

Gus, Cole, and most of their men had come down off the mountain and retreated either to their homes or to a hotel for hot showers and rest. So far, they had found no further sign of the smuggler named Tommy Cortez, and neither had Dee. She had given up as there was nothing to track and had stopped by just to tell them she didn't think they needed to worry.

The way Sam looked at it, if Dee Gallant couldn't track the man, the man didn't exist.

Dee had told him she was tracking a renegade cougar, and suggested they lock the horses in the barn for the night, especially the old donkey and Jenny's pony. The cat had killed two calves at the Diamond Bar and another neighbour's newborn foal as well.

Everything had a place in the world, Sam reckoned, whether it was wolves, cougars, cattle, or horses, but when an animal went rogue, something had to be done. If he wasn't so busy fixing up the ranch and looking after all these old people, he'd be helping Dee track the beast down.

Sam sighed, belted down the shot of whiskey, and closed his eyes.

BJ and Jenny were bringing the ranch horses in and locking them up for the night. He had good grandkids, hardworking and reliable. Little Jenny was strung tight as banjo strings, but she had a lot of heart and gave it her all when she set her mind to something.

Sam chuckled.

A reality show blared from the TV in the living room, but soon the sounds of the contestants grunting, and gasping faded away as he fell into a deep sleep.

The scrape of a ladder's extension being raised woke Sam from a deep sleep.

He stretched the kink out of his back and leaned forward. The clock on his nightstand read one a.m. He had been dead to the world for five hours.

He got up and wandered into the living room. The grandfather clock in the corner's quiet ticking sounded like the countdown to New Year's Eve in Times Square inside the sleepy house.

Once again Emma had left the light on upstairs so that the old ladies and the kids could see their way to the bathroom, but no one was about. The bathroom door stood open, the room dark inside.

A soft blue light cast a thin rectangular beam across the living room's wood planked floors. Cade always kept a night light on in his bedroom. Sam thought he saw someone moving in the shadows, the blue light blackening in places as if someone was wandering about. There was a faint rustling behind the door.

Was Cade attending to his wife?

Was that what awakened him?

Sam couldn't remember. His shoulder slouched, tiredness weighing them down.

Should he knock to see if Cade needed help with Sylvie?

Sam stood at the foot of the stairs and listened. There was no movement on the second floor and all motion had suddenly stopped inside the O'Hara's bedroom.

He shrugged, a cold draft brushing against him like a ghostly cat twining between his legs. Sam shivered.

It was all that talk of renegade cougars and smugglers that had got him going.

He chuckled to himself as he unlocked the lock on the gun rack and took down his Remington lever action 30-30. He checked the chamber. It was empty. He deposited five bullets into it and wandered over to the front door.

You can never be too careful, he thought, as he pulled on his boots and then unlocked the front door. He had put the reverse lock door handle on that afternoon to prevent Zoe from any further visits to the stable after dark.

So far, Sam breathed a sigh of relief; all were fast asleep in their respective beds.

Sam wandered out to the barn, stopping once to enjoy the starry night. Stars twinkled from horizon to horizon, except where the mountains rose high into the night. Somewhere off to the East a coyote howled.

Sam smiled.

He loved this place.

Finally, he drew back the door and walked inside. He found the light switch on the side wall and flicked it on.

The barn was warm and toasty, but not sweltering. The nights now were getting cooler as the summer was approaching its end.

Only his old cutting horse, Boomer, and the dark almost black Warmblood stallion called Midnight Special, who went by the barn name of Buddy, were up and eating hay from the manger. The rest of the horses were lying down or sleeping standing up in their respective stalls.

A series of heavy snores came from the stall beside Mary's paint stallion, Patch.

Sam laughed.

That mangy donkey could sure saw logs!

"Hey, Buddy," Sam crooned to the Hanoverian stallion. He rubbed his forelock as he glanced over the stall door.

The stallion was huge, big boned and hammer headed. His hooves were massive, bigger than a man's hand with fingers spread. Warm walnut colored eyes regarded him with calm curiosity. Sam had the distinct feeling that an old soul was looking back at him.

"What happened to your sheet," Sam asked the stallion, noting that the belly bands on his cotton quilted night rug were incorrectly tied.

Sam slid open the bolt on the door and walked inside, moving the horse over with one hand as he did so.

Normally, the belly bands crossed from front to back, so they formed an 'X' under the horse's stomach. The Hanoverian's belly bands were straight across.

"That's odd," Sam mused, stroking the horse's neck.

Jenny couldn't have done it. She didn't dare step into the stallion stalls; except for Patch's, and only if Mary was with her. BJ would never have done up the belly bands like that.

"Let's fix you up, big guy," Sam said, unfastening the hooks on the blanket.

He tugged the blanket back into place and lengthened the ties back up so he could cross them when he noticed something odd. There were no shavings or scraps of hay on the blanket. The stallion's shoulders and back were curried to a bright sheen.

"If only you could talk, eh boy," he muttered.

Sam fastened the straps, gave the stallion one last pat, and then left the stall, his brows knitting together in puzzlement.

He quietly checked on the rest of the horses and tossed an extra flake of hay into the stalls that had none, shut off the light, and slowly made his way back to the house, rifle in hand.

As he approached the veranda, he saw a flicker of movement in the O'Hara's bedroom window. He thought he saw a delicate hand let the lace curtain go, the cotton fabric falling back into place with a gentle swaying motion.

Sam grinned, remembering the words to one of his wife's favourite songs, a 'B' side song by Buffy Saint Marie:

God is alive; magic is afoot. He had the feeling that both God and magic were in play this night.

Sam continued to walk to the house, his pace slow and relaxed. If magic was afoot, it was good magic and nothing for him to be fearful of. Indeed, he wondered if a celebration wasn't in order.

He entered the house, locked the door behind him, removed the bullets from his rifle, and then locked it back in the rifle rack above the bookcase in the living room.

Once again, the house appeared quiet. There was a flurry of movement behind the O'Hara's door, but then it stilled.

Sam fought the urge to knock at said door. Instead, he kicked off his boots and crawled into bed.

He lay there in the dark for some time, hand behind his head, listening to the soft creaking of the house, the multitude of noise from the world outside, the frogs, the crickets, and the night birds. A chorus of coyotes yelped at the moon. The silvery crescent shape of the scimitar appeared to fall out of the night sky as dawn approached.

Soft footsteps echoed in the stairwell. The stair boards were too old to provide noiseless travel.

Squeak. Swoosh. Squeak. Swoosh.

The door to the O'Hara's room opened and then closed again, ever so softly.

The sound was followed by the squeaking of bed springs through the paper-thin walls.

Magic was definitely afoot, Sam realized, and more than a wee bit of hanky panky too.

Chapter Eleven

There is no secret so close as that between a rider and his horse.

The next several days were peaceful at the ranch. A routine had developed at *The Silver Spurs Home for Aging Cowgirls.* Zoe continued to teach BJ complicated dressage movements every other day. The gang of seniors spent the evenings watching TV or attentively clapping along to whatever Jenny had dreamed up for entertainment that evening. The manure pile was getting bigger and bigger with all the horses continuing to be stabled at night. Sam and BJ with a little help from a love-struck sheriff and an ATF lieutenant had fenced in five extra horse runs so that the stallions and the Andalusian filly could go out during the day. Midnight Special was getting nightly grooming by a ghostly visitor in the night.

"Think I'll head into town today," Sam declared over breakfast one morning.

"I wouldn't mind going with you, Sam," Cade said, tucking a napkin into the top of his wife's blouse. "I need to pick up a few things."

"Can I go to," Jenny chirruped balancing a spoonful of Cheerio's in midair. "I need to pick up a few things too."

"You do, do you," Emma chuckled.

"Actually, I wouldn't mind a trip into town either. I need a few supplies," Mary added.

"Maybe you can help me pick out a new cowboy hat," Cade said to Jenny.

"I'd love that," Jenny mumbled through a mouthful of cereal.

"I need to stock up as well," Emma replied, dishing out a ladle full of scrambled eggs onto BJ's plate.

"Let's make a day of it," Zoe chimed in.

"We can take my truck, it seats six comfortably," Cade offered.

"And I bet you've never ridden in a Beamer before," Zoe winked at Emma.

"With the sunroof open," Emma asked, "like that movie with Gina Davis. What was it called? You know the one where the girls wind up fugitives and drive their car over the cliff."

"Thelma and Louise, you mean," Zoe laughed. "That's a classic."

"How about we not drive any cars over a cliff though," Sam muttered.

The ladies at the table laughed.

"Sound's like a fun day," Mary exclaimed.

"Oh, dear, what about Mrs O'Hara," Emma asked worriedly.

"S'okay," BJ replied, "I'll look after her. I'd like to practice some of the things that Zoe taught me on Bucky.

Bucky's not Zippo, but he can learn all that leg bending stuff. I can wheel Mrs O'Hara out to the barn with me."

"I'm sure she'd be delighted, even if she can't say so," Cade cried, thrilled by the offer.

"That is very generous of you," Maggie said, tilting her head to one side as she examined the teen.

BJ blushed under the heavy scrutiny.

"Are you sure, honey," Emma inquired of her son.

BJ nodded and speared a piece of bacon with his fork.

"Don't worry, Emma, I'll make sure Sylvie's personal needs are taken care of before we go," Cade stated.

"I'll call granddad or you on the cell if I need help," BJ said.

"That's settled then," Mary chortled. "Road trip!"

Sam sighed. This hadn't gone as planned. He had wanted a day to himself.

He glanced sideways at Sylvie.

Sylvie's hair glistened in the beam of sunlight that shone down upon her through the window, the thin threads of coppery auburn a river of sable between the white hairs. Cade had pulled her hair back this morning and tied it behind her head. Her sky-blue eyes twinkled like blue sapphires, her delicate features smooth and refined, alabaster skin unblemished by time.

Sylvie O'Hara must have been a real head turner in her day, Sam thought.

Sylvie shivered.

Her head didn't turn, but her eyes met Sam's. Sam felt like the floor had just collapsed underneath him. Those blue eyes of hers were enchanting, the look she gave him filled with both defiance and pain.

Sam gulped down the last of his coffee, turning away before someone at the table noticed.

When he glanced back, Sylvie's head drooped forward slightly as Cade fed her. A thin smile creased her lips.

Cade turned and whispered something into Maggie's ear.

The smile disappeared instantly.

Heaven help me, Sam thought.

Sam excused himself from the table and unhooked the cell phone from its charger beside the old rotary dial telephone on the side table and slipped it into his front shirt pocket.

The trip to town proved interesting, so interesting that Sam quickly found an excuse to escape the gaggle of women as they prattled on and on about bust sizes and liposuction, dragging him first to one clothing store, then another, and then finally to a small boutique store that had just opened up. Sam made a beeline for the honky-tonk on Main Street as soon as he could.

One would have thought Cade and Jenny were off in search of pirate treasure the way they whispered conspiratorially back and forth. Sam had the feeling that he didn't want to know what that was about.

Eventually, the odd couple, the bandy legged bald old man with a sliver of ponytail falling to just below his collar and the precocious Raggedy Anne of a little girl bounded off down the street in search of a cowboy hat and only the Lord knew what else.

Sam opened the battered black door with a Budweiser sign painted on it, sauntered up to the bar, and then ordered himself a beer.

"Haven't seen you for a while, Sam," the bartender said, pouring a glass of draft from the spigot behind the bar.

"Yeah, I've been tied up," Sam drawled, placing two bills on the bar.

"Scuttle butt says you guys opened some kind of senior's home at the ranch," the bartender said, depositing the beer in front of Sam with one hand and scooping up the bills with the other.

"Yep, we did," Sam replied, staring into his beer.

"That why you're here," the bartender joked.

"Yes sir," Sam agreed.

The bartender and Sam shared a laugh.

"Heard you got an America's Most Wanted running around up in the hills behind your ranch too."

"Doubt it," Sam muttered. "If all those ATF fellas and the sheriff and state troopers couldn't find him, he's either not there or dead somewhere in a gulch."

The bartender nodded and left Sam to his beer.

Not too long afterwards, Cade pushed open the door to the saloon and joined Sam at the bar. Cade was sporting a black felt Stetson.

"So, you're gonna start cowboying now, are you," Sam said to Cade.

"If you'll teach me," Cade grinned.

Sam grunted with amusement.

"You've had both those women around you all these years and you never learned to ride," Sam quipped while Cade ordered a draft.

"Oh, I learned to ride partner, but not a horse," Cade beamed. "It was always: 'Cade, dear, be a doll and fetch me that halter', or 'Cade, do hook up the trailer and then come back and load the horses, plus don't forget the tack trunks', and 'darling, I believe we're out of wine, run to the liquor store, will you'. The best one had to be: 'Cade, Buddy's and Storm's sheathes are icky, do clean them'."

Sam burst out laughing. Nothing worse than having to clean a stallion's or a gelding's dirty sheath. He wondered why Cade didn't just call the vet and be done with it.

"Did I ever tell you about Maggie's theory on fertility," Cade drawled, leaning in close to Sam.

"Can't say that you have," Sam mumbled back, not sure he wanted to know.

"Another round, Sam," the bartender asked.

"Not for me," Sam pushed his empty glass away. "One is enough."

"One is never enough," Cade spouted, and then to the bartender, "Hit me."

The bartender drew another glass of beer and slid it across the bar to Cade.

Sam was seeing a side of Cade that Sam didn't like. That devil-may-care attitude of his was hiding something. It looked like booze was Cade's Achilles heel.

"Maggie thinks that you can tell how virile a stallion is, or a man, by the length of his dick," Cade whispered to Sam. "Can you imagine that immaculate snippety gorgeous piece of tail crawling under her stallion to measure the length of his dick? Not only that, but she did it to Sylvie's stallion as well."

Sam raised an eyebrow.

Cade wasn't serious, was he?

Cade downed his beer in two swallows and ordered a third.

"How about you give me your keys, Cade," Sam suggested, holding out his hand.

"That's probably wise," Cade smirked, handing Sam his truck keys, "although I drive better drunk than sober."

"I doubt it," Sam snapped, standing up, "and where is my granddaughter, Cade?"

"Oh, she bought herself a brand spanking new pair of riding boots at the tack store and ran off to show her mother," the newly outfitted dime store cowboy said to the real McCoy.

"Where'd she get the money to do that," Sam demanded, flustered.

"Ooooh, that granddaughter of yours is a pistol, Sam Montana," he slurred, downing a fourth beer in record time. "She's a real little venture capitalist."

Sam decided he would have a serious chat with his granddaughter when they got home.

"You know it's my fault really," Cade continued, his mood suddenly turning morose.

"What is," Sam asked, hoping he wouldn't have to carry Cade out to the truck.

"Sylvie's stroke," he sobbed into his beer.

"How so," Sam asked.

144

"It was Maggie's seventieth birthday party," Cade recalled. "The girls were running out of wine and sent me to the liquor store. I came back to find them both quite drunk, you see. Maggie confessed to sneaking into our barn to measure Buddy's dick and let it slip about our affair. Oh, Sylvie was furious. I mean, Sylvie knew, you know what I mean. We never spoke about it, but she's my wife. A woman knows, Sam. She knows when her man is sleeping around. I can't help it. It's like an itch that won't go away and until you scratch so hard you make yourself bleed. The two most beautiful women in the world are in love with me and still that's not enough."

"Yeah, well I've heard enough," Sam said gruffly, snatching the glass of draft from Cade's hand. He placed it on the bar and yanked Cade off the bar stool.

"She had the stroke right there and then... Maggie was so cruel... it broke Sylvie's heart," Cade sobbed, wrapping one arm over Sam's shoulder as if he was his best buddy.

So that was how it happened, Sam seethed. No wonder Cade's wife looked so broken – she was!

The cell phone in Sam's pocket rang.

"Hello," Sam growled, pushing Cade towards the front door while answering the call.

"You need to get home," a woman's voice whispered hoarsely over the phone.

"Who is this," Sam hissed angrily.

"Sam Montana, get home now," the voice commanded.

The line went dead as the caller hung up the phone.

Sam pushed the call display number on the cell phone. The ranch home number popped up on the screen.

Sam blanched.

He dragged Cade out of the bar and raced to the truck yelling for his daughter as she and the ladies exited the grocery store up the street pushing two shopping carts full of groceries in front of them.

BJ pushed Mrs O'Hara's wheelchair across the yard and into the shade of the barn.

"Mrs O'Hara, I'm just gonna go get Bucky and then I'll be back pronto," BJ said to the disabled woman.

BJ snatched a rope halter from a hook by one of the stalls and wandered off in search of his buckskin gelding.

Inside the barn, the stalls stood open, the ranch horses being turned out in the pasture, the donkey and the paint stallion in the large grass paddock beside the barn, and the other two stallions and the filly in their own paddocks behind the riding ring.

Sylvie relaxed in her wheelchair. Her nostrils quivered, and she closed her eyes, a wan smile creeping across her face. The smell of the horses and fresh cut hay were better than any fancy perfume to a woman raised with horses. Both of her parents had been horse lovers. Sylvie had fallen in love with God's most precious gift to mankind before she could walk.

Sylvie loved the sound of BJ's gelding's steel shoes clip-clopping across the cement floor as the teen returned, leading his Quarter horse in through one of the back doors.

"I'm just gonna saddle Bucky and I'll take you out to the riding ring where you can enjoy the sun," BJ prattled on to the silent woman, first grooming his horse and then saddling him.

"Maybe one day if you and Mr O'Hara don't mind, I can exercise Buddy for you. I'm sure he'd like to go on a trail ride. I wish you could too. It's beautiful in the mountains. The trails are endless."

BJ pushed the wheelchair down the barn aisle's and out into the sun. The large buckskin gelding followed obediently along behind him, his head relaxed, his hoofbeats muffled by the sandy earth.

"I'd say for you to tell me if'n it gets too hot, but you can't do that so I'll keep watch to make sure you don't fry," BJ said, positioning the wheelchair so that Sylvie could watch him work his horse in the ring but also so that the sun wasn't in her eyes.

BJ led his horse into the ring and closed the gate behind him. He mounted his horse and began doing some bending exercises that Zoe had taught him.

Suddenly there was a loud shriek coming from the pasture.

The ranch horses stampeded across the hayfields in a hail of flying hooves and clods of grass.

Inside Patch and Mike's pen, the donkey brayed a warning. Mary's paint stallion screamed and reared, pinning back his ears, his front feet slashing the air.

The other stallions also squealed in warning and galloped wildly about their enclosures. The filly raced up and down her fence line, trying to find a way out of her pen.

Over top of the riding ring's rails, BJ saw a giant mountain lion stalk across the yard towards the paint and donkey's pasture. It moved stealthily towards the small donkey.

BJ's horse whirled on its haunches and reared in response.

"No," BJ screamed, casting a glance from the mountain lion to the donkey, just in time to see the mountain lion leap onto Mike's back.

The buckskin wheeled around.

BJ flew threw the air, unable to stay on the frenzied gelding. He hit the ground hard, his head slamming into the dirt. Before everything went black, BJ realized the donkey didn't stand a chance and neither did Mrs O'Hara.

Sylvie heard the cougar's growl and knew instinctively that it would go for the donkey.

There was no time to think.

BJ was down, unconscious in the ring, his gelding galloping back and forth across the ring, stirrups and reins flying.

Sylvie and BJ were sitting ducks.

There were screams of anger, wails of fear, and a cacophony of growls and howls coming from the far paddock as the paint stallion valiantly galloped to the donkey's rescue.

There was no time to waste.

Sylvie sprang out of her wheelchair and staggered towards the barn. She grabbed a steel pitch fork from inside the door and hobbled back to where BJ lay motionless on the ground. She knew Sam had a couple of rifles and shotguns in the house, but retrieving them wasn't an option.

Sylvie saw the paint stallion wheel around and kick out with its hind hooves, catching the cougar in mid-air as it scrambled off the donkey's back and turned to face the stallion. The stallion whirled struck at the cougar with flying feet and teeth, its ears pinned back in rage.

"Good for you, Patches," Sylvie shouted, "get that sucker."

The stallion connected once again. The cat screamed in pain.

Sylvie stood, pitchfork at the ready, straddling the downed teen.

The cougar crawled out of the paint's way and slithered under the wooden fence rails. It licked its wounds and then looked up, catching a whiff of the old woman and the boy.

"Shit," Sylvie exclaimed.

She looked around the riding ring.

The gelding snorted, snot flying in every direction. Bucky's fear was palpable, rolling off the terrified horse in waves. The whites of his eyes were visible.

There was no help there.

Damn, if only it had been one of the other stallions in the ring.

That gave Sylvie an idea. She didn't know if it would work, but it was worth a try.

"Move," she yelled at the frightened gelding, waving her arms in the air to chase him out of her way.

She slid open the latch on the cattle pens and raced in. Her stallion and Maggie's stallion's paddocks were on the far side. She threw open the door to the Hanoverian's pen.

"Come here, Buddy," she called to her horse.

The stallion whinnied and galloped to her.

"Good boy," she crooned.

She led him through the cattle pen by the halter and let him loose in the riding ring. She knew that he would avoid trampling BJ just like the gelding did. Even in a panic, the horses wouldn't hurt the teen.

"Go get him," she commanded.

The cougar jumped over the top fence rail and into the ring, slinking towards the downed boy.

"Git! Get out of here," she screamed, racing across the ring and waving her arms in the air. Her legs shook with the effort. She hadn't been walking for long. Her stallion and the gelding followed close behind her.

Sylvie reached the boy, snatched the metal pitch fork off the ground and faced the cougar, standing legs spread, like a gladiator facing a lion in Rome's coliseum.

Sylvie thought her heart would explode in her chest; it was beating so furiously against her ribcage. Her breathing came sharp and ragged. It had been five years since she'd done this much activity.

"Go on, git you son of a gun," she growled facing the cougar.

The cougar padded towards her, its paws huge, its talons digging into the sandy earth. Sylvie stabbed the air in front of it.

The cougar snarled and crouched, readying itself to spring.

Blood matted its shoulder where the paint stallion had sunk its teeth into the cougar's hide.

Sylvie braced for the impact, knowing that she was too old and too tiny to withstand the weight of a pouncing mountain lion, but she was damned if she wasn't going to go down swinging.

All at once, her enormous bay stallion charged by her. The stallion leapt into the air and all sixteen hundred pounds of him crashed down atop the cougar in a flurry of slashing hooves and snapping teeth. Dappled bay and sable coat intermingled as the stallion and the cougar collided. The cougar leapt out of the way a split second before one of the stallion's hooves shattered its skull.

With a flick of its tail, the cat decided it had enough. It leapt over the wood railed fence in a single bound, and fled across the pasture as fast as its legs could carry it.

"And that's why they call him The Midnight Special," Sylvie wailed, shaking a fist at the retreating cougar.

The stallion's neck glistened with sweat. His entire body trembled with adrenaline. The bay snorted, his black nostrils flaring. He then let out a triumphant whinny.

Sylvie winced and covered her ears.

The gelding trotted over to sniff the stallion. He licked his lips in submission.

The tall Hanoverian horse nosed Sylvie's hand. She threw her arms around his neck and hugged him close.

"I am so proud of you," she crooned.

The gelding nudged her arm.

"What? You didn't do anything," she chastised the buckskin and then broke down, giving the gelding a hug too.

"Okay, move off you two," she said, pushing the pair of horses out of the way.

She bent down to check on BJ. The boy was deathly pale. He moaned when she pinched one of his fingers.

"Well that's a good sign," Sylvie murmured. "You two guard him while I go call for help."

The horses snorted out an answer.

Sylvie hurried to the riding ring's gate and pushed it open. Her muscles ached from disuse. She quickly ran out of breath, exhaustion weighing her down as she hurried to the house.

A stitch ripped through her side.

She grimaced and walked on.

Sylvie slid the screen door open and dashed into the kitchen. She rifled through the papers beside the phone until she found the phone number she was looking for.

What was she doing, Sylvie asked herself, holding the receiver in one hand? The dial tone buzzed like an angry fly.

That darned cowboy would know it was her.

Would he keep her secret?

"Oh, Hades, he knows anyway," she muttered to herself as she dialled Sam's cell number.

Chapter Twelve

To ride on a horse is to fly without wings.

Sam drove into the yard with only Emma and Cade in the truck. The three ladies had treated themselves and Jenny out to lunch. Cade was too drunk to join them.

Sam's mood was dour as he parked Cade's big dually truck in front of the barn.

Emma anxiously chewed on her lower lip.

Cade snored, asleep in the back seat amidst twenty plus bags of groceries.

"You run up to the house and I'll check out back," Sam told his daughter-in-law as he unbuckled his seat belt.

All seemed quiet as he stepped out of the truck.

"You really don't know who called?" Emma croaked.

Sam shook his head and strode off towards the barn, leaving Emma behind.

He heard muffled footfalls behind him as Emma jogged up to the ranch house calling: "BJ! BJ, are you in the house?"

Sam looked towards the larger mountain in the range that stretched from northeast to northwest that bordered the valley and his far pastures. He could see the ranch horses grazing in the distance. That was odd as they usually grazed in the lower pasture closer to the ranch house and the little brook that ran through to it.

"BJ," he called as he stepped into the barn.

The stall doors were all closed. There were no horses inside the barn.

He opened the door to the tack room and noticed BJ's cutting saddle wasn't on its rack.

Sam exited the rear door of the barn. A horse nickered softly to him from inside the riding ring. It was BJ's buckskin, still saddled, reins looped around its neck. Beside the buckskin stood Sylvie's big boned bay Hanoverian stallion. The stallion looked up, nonchalantly checking him out, its colossal body shading both the woman in the wheelchair and the boy on the ground.

"BJ," Sam gasped seeing his grandson sitting on the ground holding his head in his hands, Sylvie O'Hara, in her wheelchair, pulled up beside him.

"Grandpa," BJ stuttered, looking towards the lean figure striding quickly towards him. "You gotta check on Mike and Patch. A cougar tried to take Mike down. I don't know if he did or not."

Sam paled when he saw the cougar tracks in the sand footing of the ring, the clear signs of a battle, and the metal tined pitchfork lying at Sylvie's feet.

"Sweet Lord," he said, squatting beside his grandson.

Sam ran a hand through his grandson's black hair, looking for injuries. Relief flooded through him. There was no blood. He then put a hand to the teen's forehead.

"I'm okay, just a little woozy," BJ groaned. "Please go check on Mrs O'Hara and Mike."

"Mrs O'Hara is right beside you," Sam said, nodding towards the silent woman sitting tall in the wheelchair. Sylvie smiled triumphantly; her gaze fixed on Sam's lined face.

"Thank you," he mouthed to the woman. She nodded imperceptibly back.

"How'd she get here," BJ said, squinting up at Sylvie.

"Magic and miracles," Sam mumbled.

Sylvie grinned, but then wiped it off her face quickly when Emma ran into the riding ring.

"BJ," Emma wailed, embracing her son. "What happened?"

"The cougar tried to get Mike," BJ cried.

And you too, Sam thought to himself.

"I'll go check on Mike and Patch," Sam replied, standing up. "You stay with them."

"How'd Mrs O'Hara's stallion get in here," Emma asked, looking over at the two horses.

"Guess he broke out of his pen and got in through the cattle pen gate," Sam replied a little sheepishly.

"And why is Mrs O'Hara in the riding ring," Emma cried out again.

"I can't answer that, Emma," Sam replied. "I'm going to check on the donkey."

Sam picked up the pitchfork, dashed to the gate, opened it, and locked it behind him. He was glad Emma hadn't asked about that.

He didn't know what happened here, but he was thankful that Sylvie O'Hara wasn't as handicapped as she pretended to be. She was an incredibly brave woman, protecting his grandson with nothing but a manure fork and an aged stallion to back her up.

The thought of what happened in the ring chilled him to the bone.

Sam reached the paint stallion and the donkey's paddock. Both trotted to greet him at the gate as if they had a story to tell him.

Dried blood the color of black berry wine covered the stallion's white nose. There was another patch of dried blood on his shoulder.

Sam checked the paint stud all over, but he couldn't find any wounds.

He then checked the one eared donkey and found a piece of broken tooth embedded in a bite mark in his back and four deep cuts along each shoulder where the cougar's four claws had dug in on either side. The wounds were slick with drying blood.

"You're lucky to be alive, old man," Sam told the donkey, pulling the piece of tooth out of the wound on his back and examining it. The tooth was about one inch long and sharply pointed at the end.

The donkey brayed pitifully.

Sam rubbed the donkey's and the paint horse's nose. The donkey would live.

Sam breathed a sigh of relief. Jenny and Mary would have been devastated if either of these animals had been killed.

Sam moved the animals aside and squatted down in the dirt around the water bucket. The cat's tracks were deep, the right paw turning slightly in. The stallion's tracks mostly obliterated the cat's, his hooves landing so hard that they dug three inches into the hard-packed summer ground. There had been quite the battle, both in the paint and donkey's pen and in the riding ring.

Sam had resented all the stallions coming to live with them, but now not so much.

He stood up and with one last rub of the donkey and paint's forelocks, went up to the house to call an ambulance for BJ, the vet for Mike, and the sheriff and Dee Gallant, the Ranger. This may or may not be the cougar that Dee was tracking, either way it was dangerous and needed to be put down.

"Emma," Sam called to his daughter-in-law who sat in the sand between her son and Sylvie, "I'm heading to the house to call an ambulance and Cole. Stay put. I'll be right back."

"Is Mike okay," she yelled back.

"He's fine," Sam hollered back.

"I don't need an ambulance, Grandpa," BJ whined.

"Yes, you do," Emma told her son.

Sam wished he could stay there in case the cougar was still around, but there was no cell service on the ranch. They only used their two cell phones when they were in town or for the kids to tell them if they would be late getting home from school.

Zoe zig-zagged her little black Beamer in between a convoy of trucks pulling horse trailers as she sped along the highway to the ranch, sunroof open, the sun beating down upon the heads of Jenny and Mary tightly in the back seat.

"You know I got to get me one of those Oprah suits," Mary said, lifting her face to catch the sun.

"A what," Maggie asked, turning in her seat.

"An Oprah suit," Mary replied. "Like she had on her show, the thing that defies gravity and pushes all the parts back to where they used to be."

"You mean a body glove," Zoe said, and then burst out laughing.

"What's that," Jenny asked innocently.

"It's a suit that when your body parts sag puts your boobs back in the right place and tightens up your bootie," Maggie guffawed.

"I'd give anything to have a body like you two," Mary quipped, meaning Zoe and Maggie.

"You don't need no help with that, Mary, I think your real pretty," Jenny said, reaching over to hug the old cowgirl.

"Oh, you're such a dear," Mary said, hugging the little girl back.

"Now I've heard everything," Zoe marveled.

The ladies all giggled as they traveled along the highway in the fancy black Beamer.

"I wonder where they're all headed," Maggie mused from the front passenger seat. She removed her dark sunglasses to get a better view of the cowboy driving a rusted Dodge pickup truck with two ranch horses poking their noses out of an equally rusty stock trailer behind it.

"Maybe there's a rodeo somewhere," Jenny said excitedly.

"Maybe we should yell out the window and invite that handsome fellow home for a game of strip poker," Mary joked, covering Jenny's ears.

"Oh, strip poker, I haven't played that in years," Maggie chortled.

"You? Strip poker? Saints alive," Zoe quipped, flooring the Beamer to pass the pickup truck.

"I love strip poker, but it's only fun if you've got some hot bodied male on the other side of the table to play with," Maggie purred.

The day out with the girls had done Maggie Carroll a lot of good, Zoe mused. Now all they had to do was pry her out from beneath Cade. If Maggie thought no one knew about her affair with Cade and their midnight escapades, she was wrong.

Zoe grinned, feeling a tad cattie.

"Why don't we have a go tonight," Zoe suggested. "We'll invite Cade. I'm sure he'll be up to it."

"Believe me, you don't want to do that," Maggie guffawed. "In the old days, yes, Cade was downright irresistible, but now not so much, if you know what I mean. Everything has gotten a little droopy."

"Honey, at our age, all of us have gotten a little droopy," Zoe chortled, "but at least you're getting some."

"I suppose," Maggie drawled, placing her sunglasses back onto her nose.

"Don't bother asking Sam, he'd never do it," Mary quipped from the back seat.

"Grandpa won't do what," Jenny queried, removing Mary's hands from over her ears.

"Nothing you'd be interested in, young lady," Zoe replied, looking Jenny in the eye via the rear-view mirror.

Jenny made a funny face.

Zoe playfully stuck out her tongue.

"Isn't that the sheriff's Suburban up ahead," Zoe said.

"Sure looks like it," Jenny replied, leaning forward.

"Why are all those trucks pulling into the ranch, I wonder," Mary asked. "We're not having a rodeo."

"Hey, we should do that," Jenny howled with glee.

"Not today, honey," Mary replied, tickling Jenny into submission.

"Guess we'll find out soon enough," Maggie purred.

"I think we should ask a couple of those hotties in for dinner," Zoe joked.

"That would be spicy," Maggie giggled.

Zoe followed the sheriff's SUV and horse trailer up the lane. Several trucks and trailers were in the yard already, about twenty men and their horses milling about. Another five trucks and trailers pulled in behind the Beamer.

Zoe parked the car in front of the ranch house. She and the rest of the gang crawled out of the sports car.

Jenny raced across the yard to where her grandfather had saddled up his reining horse, Checkers. The sorrel gelding was alert; its ears pricked forward, head up, eyes bright with anticipation.

"Grandpa, what's going on," Jenny yelled, skidding to a stop in front of her grandfather.

Her grandfather raised a hand, shushing her, as he talked quietly to a fellow rancher.

The ladies gathered their bags of purchases from the back of the car and strolled towards the house. Emma and Dee came out to greet them.

"Emma, what on earth is all the fuss," Mary asked keenly.

"First, I want to tell you that all your horses are fine," Emma replied calmly. "I locked them in the barn along with all the ranch horses."

"What do you mean by that," Maggie snapped. "If anything has happened to Storm, I'll sue you into bankruptcy."

"Calm down, Maggie," Zoe told the angry woman. "Emma just said the horses are fine."

"Nothing has happened to Storm, or Buddy, or Patch, or the Andalusians, Zoe," Emma said. "Only BJ and Mike got hurt, but they'll be okay too."

"Oh, my God, Emma," Mary gasped.

"It was a cougar," Dee explained. "It's the same one that I've been hunting for two weeks. He's taken down a few cattle in the area, but now he's graduated to newborn foals and donkeys."

Mary's hand flew to cover her mouth.

The old horsewomen paled at the thought.

Jenny wailed in the front yard as her grandfather told her of Mike's injuries. Sam wrapped his arms around his granddaughter and hugged her close.

"The vet has been and gone," Emma assured the women. "Mike has some deep cuts, and he's on antibiotics for a while, but he has survived worse than a cougar bite."

"But he was in the same pen as Patch," Mary said, her face whitening even more.

"From the tracks in the paddock, your stallion took a good chunk out of the cougar before sending him packing," Dee said, purposefully leaving out Sam's telling her about all the blood he washed off the stallion. "There's not a scratch on Patch."

Mary sat down with a heavy thump on one of the porch chairs. She let out a great sigh of relief.

Emma took some of the bags from the ladies' hands and tried to escort them into the house, but they were having none of it.

"You said BJ was hurt," Zoe stammered. "The cougar attacked him too?"

"No, he got knocked unconscious when he fell off Bucky, but he's okay. He's resting upstairs," Emma replied. "Cade is watching over him."

"What about Sylvie," Maggie shouted hysterically. "Wasn't BJ going to take her out to get some air?"

"She's fine too. She's resting right now as well," Emma told them.

"I gotta go," Dee said, nodding a thank you to Emma. "With all the help I have, I should be able to track that cat down easily."

The silver haired women watched the men gathered in the yard check their rifles and then pop them into the scabbards attached to their saddles. There were over thirty grim-faced men ready to ride out.

"Seriously, ladies, this is a one-off incident. You don't get rogue cats like this often," Dee said.

"That's what the sheriff said about Mexican crime lords falling from the sky," Zoe mumbled.

"Please, come in the house," Emma begged the ladies. "I've got tea and coffee on."

"Have anything stronger," Mary trembled.

"Will a shot of Johnny Walker do," Emma said, forcing a smile.

"It'll help," the old cowgirl replied.

Sam, Dee, Cole, and all the ranchers, ranging in age from seventeen to seventy-eight, mounted on their colourful assortment of horses from chestnuts to bays, paints to appaloosas, and blacks to greys, trotted off, three and four abreast, through the gate leading to the Montana ranch's high pastures. A tearful red-haired Jenny stood in a cloud of dust waving them on.

"You don't see that every day," Zoe gushed.

"Part of me wants to ride out with them," Mary agreed.

"Me too," Emma mumbled.

"To hunt down a cougar," Maggie said, casting a sour glance Mary's way. "You must be mad."

"Oh, Maggie, where's your spirit of adventure," Zoe chortled.

"In the house with that bottle of Johnny Walker," Maggie drawled.

Chapter Thirteen

*Horses change lives. They give our young people confidence and
self-esteem. They provide peace and tranquility to troubled souls
- they give us hope.*
Toni Robinson

The men came back that night tired and exhausted. Dee
had tracked the cat through several small stream
tributaries, but then lost it on a shale slope. Despite the
men fanning out into six separate groups, they couldn't
find hide or hair of the rogue mountain lion or the Mexican
drug runner and smuggler's body.

Sam sat rocking on the porch, watching the lights from
the last trailer disappear up the lane and then turn north
onto the main highway. The men would be back in the
morning, ready to hunt the illusive cougar once more.

The moon rose in the sky. The sunset was a firestorm of
red, orange and yellow. Out in the mountains, it was easy
to imagine Apollo driving his golden chariot across the sky
at sundown, his team of white horses elegantly pulling the
chariot across the Heavens.

Sam rocked and stewed, drank his coffee, and thought about how lucky he was. BJ was alive. Sylvie O'Hara deserved a medal for bravery, her incredible stallion too for that matter.

He sighed. He had a tough decision to make.

Cade had paid for three months in advance. The money had come in handy, but Cade's morals were questionable.

He knew that Sylvie O'Hara had suffered a major stroke and, in some ways, understood, or thought he understood, why she hadn't let her husband know about her recovery.

Cade O'Hara was a drunk. Sam saw Cade taking out the empty bottles of wine and spirits from his room when he thought no one could see, carefully storing the empties in his horse trailer's living quarters. Sam liked a shot of whiskey at night or a beer on a sweltering summer's day, but only one.

Sam supposed he could deal with that, talk to him man to man, but Cade had brought his long-time mistress with him to a retirement home. Cade's devotion to his wife was admirable but rubbing his infidelities in her face under Sam's roof was unforgivable and against the Seventh Commandment.

And yet, Cade had watched over BJ most of the afternoon, entertaining his grandson with games of cards. Sylvie, Emma had told him, had slept most of the afternoon.

Sylvie O'Hara made Sam's heart quicken. She was the first woman to do that since he had met his future wife, Adelaide, at a Houston rodeo thirty-eight years ago. Adelaide had been the daughter of the livestock agent who supplied the bulls and broncs to the rodeo circuit. Adelaide was fearless. Her raven hair and deep brown eyes had set his nerves on fire.

Sylvie's audacity and sheer bravado was comparable to Adelaide's own. He suspected the two women would have been fast friends if they had met.

Sam's heart broke.

Should he keep Sylvie's secret?

What would the repercussions be if he revealed her secret?

What would it do to his family?

"Grandpa, can I go check on Mike," his granddaughter asked, pushing open the porch screen door.

Sam started and then broke into a grin when he saw the freckled-faced red-headed child looking up at him expectantly, clad in Whinny the Pooh pajamas and sparkling knee-high black leather riding boots, her grey eyes twinkling.

"Come here, sweetheart," he said, patting his knee. His granddaughter wasn't old enough not to want to cuddle with her grandfather anymore. Sam rued the day that would happen. He suspected it would hit him like a freight train when it did.

Jenny climbed onto his lap.

"Now, why don't you tell me about where you got the money to buy those boots," Sam scolded the child gently.

"I went into business," she chirped.

"You went into business, did you?"

"Uh-huh," Jenny blushed.

"How about we start again," Sam urged her. "Who did you go into business with?"

"Cade," she whispered.

"I see," he said gruffly. "And what does this business relationship entail?"

"Keeping a secret," she said, her lower lip quivering.

"Does this family keep secrets?"

"No, sir."

"And are you going to continue to keep secrets for Mr O'Hara?"

"No, sir."

"Are we going to have this conversation ever again," Sam continued.

"No, sir."

"Okay, go put something on over your pj's and we'll go check on your donkey," Sam chortled.

Jenny threw her arms around his neck and kissed him on the cheek. Sam laughed.

"I love you, Grandpa," she whispered in her grandfather's ear.

"I love you too, Jenny-penny," he replied, his voice catching in his throat as he did so.

Upstairs, Cade knocked politely on Zoe's door. Zoe threw the door open to greet him. She also wore knee high black leather riding boots, but nothing else except for a black top hat and a lascivious grin.

Cade's mouth fell open in a big round 'O'.

"You are such a wicked boy," Zoe whispered in his ear, crooking her finger in a come-hither motion.

Cade snapped his mouth shut.

"Yes, ma'am," he whispered back, closing the door softly behind him.

Across the hall, the door to Maggie's room opened a crack.

Sam walked his granddaughter back from the barn. All was well. The horses and dog-eared donkey were safe in their stalls behind closed doors.

"Now, you head straight to bed," he told his granddaughter. "It's getting late."

"Okay, Grandpa," she cooed, skipping along beside him.

Sam felt his heart swell. Despite the hard times, he was a lucky man.

Tomorrow was another day, he thought. Tomorrow he would decide what to do about the two O'Hara's and Maggie Carroll.

The lights were still on in the house, both upstairs and down, all except for Mary's and Zoe's rooms. He could see Emma finishing the last of the dishes in the kitchen and a small hand pulling back the curtains in the O'Hara's bedroom. Sylvie lifted a hand in greeting, her tiny hand not much bigger than his granddaughter's. She then stepped back and let the curtain fall back into place.

Sam's breath caught in this throat. Cade must already be upstairs in Maggie's room.

"You okay, Grandpa," Jenny asked innocently.

"Just a frog in my throat," he croaked.

"Ribbit, ribbit," Jenny said, bending down and hopping the rest of the way across the yard like a frog.

Sam laughed; the spell breaking.

Cade and Sylvie O'Hara needed a talking to. Emma had a waiting list. He was sure the O'Hara's and Miss Carroll wouldn't be too hard to replace, and for the sake of his soul he needed to remove the temptation that was Sylvie O'Hara.

It was a conundrum, he mused. If someone had told him he'd become smitten with another man's wife, he'd have called them a dirty liar.

He clung to his granddaughter's hand as they climbed the two stairs up to the porch, Jenny still hopping along like a frog.

"Nighty-night, sweetheart," he said, scooting the big frog up the stairs.

"Goodnight, Grandpa," Jenny replied. "Good night, Mom."

"Goodnight, honey," Emma replied from the kitchen.

"I'm off too, Emma," Sam called to his daughter-in-law.

"See you in the morning, Dad," Emma hollered back.

Sam stopped short. His eyes glistened with tears. That was the first time Emma had ever called him 'Dad'.

He wiped his eyes and then walked on, treading lightly so as not to disturb anyone.

He was looking forward to a good night's sleep. His back and knees were killing him. "Getting old isn't for the faint of heart," his mother used to say, and she was right.

Emma scrubbed the counter around the kitchen sink with the ferocity of a hurricane. Her fingers were raw; her hands chapped. Sweat dripped down her face.

The last two weeks had caught up to her: crazy seniors, stallions galore, a one eared donkey, a plane crash, a smuggler on the run, a posse of gun wielding ATF agents, state troopers, Cole and his deputies, Gus Rodriquez's arrival, a rogue mountain lion, her son's near death experience, and then a hunting party filled with every neighbour for twenty miles around.

She would have to hire a cook's helper and cleaning woman as she couldn't keep up with all the cooking, dirty dishes, and visitors.

Emma stopped for a minute and looked at her reflection in the kitchen window. She looked like a harried housewife. Her face was flushed, her eyes black rimmed, and her hair hung in wet ringlets around her face. She had aged ten years in fourteen days.

Her stomach growled. Acid rose unbidden into her throat. She leaned over the sink.

That was what jealousy did to you, she chastised herself.

When she saw her friend Dee riding out beside Cole in search of the cougar, a pretty smile on her lips, Emma had fought the irresistible urge to race across the pasture and pull Dee out of the saddle and throttle her. She had envied the brown-haired Ranger – her freedom, her worry-free lifestyle, her job. The list seemed endless.

Emma pushed herself away from the sink.

She tackled the stove next, pushing her violent thoughts aside.

She liked Mary and so did the kids. Mary easily adjusted to living at the ranch, but then Mary was a true cowgirl, and a wonderful cowgirl grandma for Jenny.

Emma had also taken a real liking to Zoe. Zoe was a bit out there, what with having outlived four husbands and divorced two. She couldn't imagine having to deal with that. At least Zoe had lightened up. She seemed to have stopped chasing her father-in-law over the past few days; although Sam took it with good humour and BJ was blossoming under her tutelage.

Emma chuckled. Zoe and Mary were keepers.

The other three were a chore. Even though Cade looked after his wife, Emma found her a constant worry and she wondered just how handicapped the woman was? She had caught her smiling and smothering a laugh on several occasions. And how did she get into the ring today from outside when BJ swears he left her in her wheelchair close to the riding ring's gate?

Cade was a force unto nature. He stank of booze in the morning, but at least he hid it from the kids. He winked much more than any man should, laughed off awkward situations, and was a womanizer. It was obvious he was having an affair with Maggie, and in the Montana house to boot. That was worse than rude; it was disrespectful.

And then there was Maggie. That woman would drive anyone to drink. She was snide, flippant, self-absorbed, and stunningly beautiful at seventy-five.

Oh, Heavens, she was jealous of her too, Emma gasped.

Exhaustion overwhelmed her, and she cried. Her endurance was at its limit.

Emma sat down heavily at the kitchen table.

The house was quiet.

Everyone but Emma had gone to bed.

Emma wished fervently that Cleve's old Border collie was still alive, and Cleve too. She'd give anything to ruffle the dog behind the ears and cuddle up on the couch with the Border collie at her feet, her husband by her side, a wonderful book, and a cup of tea. Throwing a puppy into the household now though would be too much, even though BJ and Jenny had been hounding her for years to get another one.

Emma sighed and rubbed her weary neck.

"Get a grip, that's not what's really bothering you and you know it," she scolded herself.

She liked Gus. He had phoned twice today to make sure that she and the kids were all right. Gus was a gorgeous hunk of man that made her heart go flip-flop. He adored the kids, and the kids adored him.

Gus had come out of the shadows. What he saw in her, she didn't know. She knew that he loved his job. She could see it in his eyes when he talked to his men. They loved and respected him back as well. Being an ATF lieutenant though was dangerous work.

Gus' job was far more dangerous than being a sheriff in a small rural mountain town.

She stood up and slowly climbed the stairs to her bedroom, head down, every step harder than the one before it.

Emma stopped, a hand on the bedroom door, pushing it open.

That was it!

She could never compete with his job. It was who Gus Rodriquez was—a soldier, a hunter of men, protector of everything he holds dear. She couldn't bury another husband, and Gus' job made that a distinct possibility. In reality, she wasn't jealous of Gus, but she was of The Cole Trane, as they used to call the sheriff in high school.

Cole was solid. He was a good-hearted man, cute like a Golden Retriever puppy, and just plain nice. He was handsome in his own way, not rugged like Gus, but athletic all the same. Cole was familiar and had even played for the Dallas Cowboys as a tight end for two seasons until a football injury knocked him to the sidelines and he came home and ran for sheriff. She had known Cole all her life. He too was one of her husband's best friends.

Yep, Emma laughed guiltily. She was jealous of Dee Gallant and Gus' love for his job. Only one of those two things really mattered.

Chapter Fourteen

*Horse sense is the thing a horse has which keeps
it from betting on people.*
W.C Fields

Maggie paced furiously around her room.

How could he?

How could Cade cheat on her? And with that scrawny needle haired bimbo! Of all people, why Zoe Puddicombe?

Sylvie was Maggie's best friend. Cade sleeping with Maggie was a given. They were family. What was the big deal? Sleeping with another woman other than Maggie and Sylvie was outrageous!

How dare he?

Maggie simmered. Her hands clenched and unclenched. Her eyes blazed with hatred for Zoe. Her anger at Cade reached the boiling point.

Maggie had been nice today. She thought she had bonded with the girls over lunch, even that dreadfully challenging child. It wasn't that Jenny wasn't adorable in her own way, Maggie simply had no use for children.

Maggie tossed a black and red nightgown over her Valentine's Day red negligee.

She would make them pay… both of them.

Maggie braced herself to let loose with a hurricane of fury when suddenly the door to her bedroom quietly opened. Cade stood in the doorway staring at her, his rheumy grey eyes slightly bloodshot, his nose Rudolph red.

Maggie smiled.

The rat!

Had she been sane at that moment, her reflection in the dresser mirror would have given her pause to reconsider her next move, but the malice that glittered in her eyes and consumed her soul from within, obliterated all sense of reason and remained unseen, all except for Cade.

Cade saw it and took a step back.

Maggie took aim and fired.

She pulled Cade into the room and slammed the door shut.

"Mags," Cade stuttered.

Maggie smiled crookedly.

"Cade," she replied seductively.

Cade half-smiled, unsure whether he was in trouble or about to get doubly laid.

Maggie released her rage!

She jumped on Cade, wrapping both hands around his throat and both legs around his body, like a python intent on squeezing the life out of him.

They toppled to the ground, Maggie on top, Cade struggling for freedom beneath her.

If he hadn't polished off a bottle of wine with Zoe, he may have stood a chance at fighting off the enraged woman, but Maggie's adrenaline was on high and Cade's fuel tank was empty.

Zoe burst into the room.

"Maggie, stop," she hissed, trying to remove the woman's hands from around her lover's throat.

Maggie back handed Zoe. The resounding slap sent Zoe careening across the room. She landed on the bed, rolling sideways from the sheer force of the blow.

Maggie continued to strangle her cheating lover.

"Stopppp," Zoe croaked. Her voice was raspy, barely above a whisper.

Cade's face went slack. His barrel chest stopped heaving, his lungs collapsing from the lack of air. His lips took on a bluish tinge. His hands fell limply away.

Startled, Maggie sat back on her haunches, gasping for breath, her fury spent.

"Oh my God, you've killed him," Zoe stammered, propping herself up on the bed.

"He deserved it," Maggie whined. "He shouldn't have cheated on me."

"Oh, but it was okay for him to cheat on his wife with you all these years," Zoe quipped.

"That was different. Sylvie and I shared everything."

"I doubt she ever expected to share her husband."

Maggie shrugged.

"What are we going to do," Zoe whispered. "You'll go to jail for life, or worst hang for it. I don't know what they do to killers here."

"I am not going to jail," Maggie seethed, "especially not for this cheating bastard. Who would take care of Storm? He'd be put down. I can't have that. And who would look out for Sylvie? I'd never abandon Sylvie."

"Let's go to my room and think about what to do," Zoe said, pushing off the bed. "I need a drink."

"What have you got," Maggie asked.

"Merlot."

"I've got something better."

Maggie stood up, tripped over her prone lover, righted herself like the lady she was, opened her nightstand and grabbed a bottle of Courvoisier Brandy, and then lifted it up in the air for Zoe's inspection.

"That will do," Zoe said, stumbling from the room.

Maggie followed her, bottle of brandy in hand. She gently tugged the door closed behind her.

Sylvie heard the commotion in the bedroom above her head. Maggie didn't realize that Sylvie and Cade's bedroom was directly below hers. Sylvie had heard every torrid sex marathon between Maggie and Cade since they all moved into *The Silver Spurs home for Aging Cowgirls*. She also heard every word the women just said.

Sylvie crept out of bed, peeked out the door to make sure Sam wasn't about, and quietly climbed the stairs.

She pressed an ear to Zoe's door, but the two women spoke too softly to hear, or they were too busy drinking. She pushed on Maggie's bedroom door. It popped open. She then carefully closed it behind her.

Sylvie stood looking down at her deceased husband. The emptiness that enveloped her surprised her. There was nothing, no remorse, no pity, no anger, just a yawning cavern filled with poisoned air. She thought back to the beginning of the end and remembered how she got here.

Sylvie O'Hara stared across the table at her old friend and nemesis, Maggie Carroll, as if she'd gone mad. A bottle of red Merlot stood empty between them; another bottle was three quarters gone. Their wine glasses were empty once again, although Sylvie couldn't remember drinking her last one. There were only two small orange cubes of cheddar cheese and one slice of dill pickle left on the tray of canapes. The sandwiches were long since depleted, as were seven other bottles of Chablis, Cabernet-Sauvignon, and one lone bottle of Champagne.

It was Maggie's seventieth birthday. She had insisted that there be no birthday cake. What Maggie wanted Maggie got, so no one had brought one.

All the guests except for Sylvie had made their excuses and gone home, tired of Maggie's callous flippancy as she got deeper into the bottle. Sylvie would have left too, but her husband had gone to the liquor store over an hour ago for more wine and still hadn't returned. She had also never seen her friend drink so much. Maggie wasn't taking seventy well.

"I'm telling you; Storm's sperm count exceeds your Midnight Special's by a hundred to one," Maggie drawled. "Its obvious, darling, that despite his age, my Desert Storm is still virile and the far better stallion of the two."

Her ultra-classy friend's behaviour surprised Sylvie. While Maggie was known for her barbed words, she rarely resulted to crudity.

Well, Sylvie thought, she could be crude when pushed too.

"You don't know that Maggie," Sylvie said, coming to the defence of her Hanoverian stallion, by using her empty wine glass as a pointer stick. "How could you really? Have you yanked my stallion off and performed a sperm count by hand?"

Maggie rolled her eyes at her friend as if she was the one who was mad.

"Ahhh, Miss Sylvia, I have my ways," the brash salt and pepper raven haired woman murmured. "Where is your husband, anyway? We're almost out of wine."

"He'll be along soon, I'm sure."

"Are you? Are you really?"

Sylvie glared at her friend. Whatever did she mean by that?

Sylvie examined her friend's face. Maggie was still a handsome woman, thanks in large part to her heritage. She was a stunningly beautiful woman in her youth; the boys had fallen over her left and right. Maggie's heritage was Native American, Spanish and Irish, her features blending the best genes in all of them, the result of which was a sultry beauty with coffee cream skin, silky black hair, and deep and unfathomable dark brown eyes. Drunk, however, her eyelids drooped, and her jowls hung down like an iguana's.

Sylvie's own salt and pepper auburn hair and sky-blue eyes were pale in comparison. In fact, the kids at high school had nicknamed them Salt and Pepper as they were inseparable as teens. Using that term now would be politically incorrect, Sylvie supposed.

"You need to be more careful with your words, Maggie, someone might take offence and never speak to you again," Sylvie jokingly replied as she refilled her glass, *"especially when it concerns their pride and joy."*

What was keeping Cade?

"All right, I'll tell you how I can prove my stallion is better than yours," Maggie said, sticking her chin defiantly up in the air.

Maggie reached under the table for her purse, an outrageously priced and rather hideous leather Gucci bag with the Gucci trademark stamped on it. She nearly went headfirst into the wall. She righted herself in a flurry of drunken movements the envy of any Navy corpsman and then yanked the Gucci bag open. She pulled out a small black and yellow measuring tape.

"I measured him," she yelled triumphantly, pulling the tape out of its holder and then letting the tape snap back in with a scratchy click.

"You what?"

"I measured him," Maggie sneered.

"You can't be serious," Sylvie flared, shocked at her friend's audacity. Even for Maggie, this was over the top.

"I snuck into your yard last year and measured the length of his dick. Your Midnight's Johnny is two inches shorter than my Storm's. It's all relative. Everyone knows, the bigger the dick, the better the chances of the mare's catching on the first go," the drunken woman replied.

Sylvie was struck dumb.

How on earth could she reply to that?

Sylvie felt herself flush. She positively burned with fury. How could this woman who called herself a friend sit there and confess that she had sneaked like a thief in the night into Sylvie's stable to jerk off her horse so she could measure the length of his willie?

Maggie and Sylvie had been rivals in the show ring for almost sixty years. They had celebrated victories and turned defeats into gales of laughter. They had signed each other's casts in the hospital when they had broken legs and arms and fed each other's horses when one or the other of them was bedridden with the flu. In short, they had laughed and cried together, hated each other and loved each other, all in equal measures. That was the biggest reason for Sylvie not tossing their friendship to the curb as many others had, women and men alike. This, however, was a joke gone too far.

Cade chose that moment to burst into the house with a bottle of red wine in one hand and a bottle of white in the other, a cheerful grin on his face. The look in his wife's eye brought him to a dead stop.

"Did I return at a bad time," he asked with some cheek.

"Maggie was just telling me how she sneaked into our yard and broke into Midnight's stall to measure the length of his willie," Sylvie grimaced, pushing away from the table. The room canted sideways.

Cade placed the bottles of wine on a side table and ran to his wife's side.

"What on ever for, Mags," he asked the woman smiling triumphantly up at him from the kitchen table as he steadied his wife's forward momentum with both hands.

"Because I can, my love. Do you know why all the mares love my stud? Well, let me tell you. His dick should be entered into the Guinness World Book of Records. It is twenty-one inches long when he's got a hard on, while your pour sod's is only

eighteen inches," Maggie finished with a giggle, opening and closing the tape measure seductively.

"Maggie," Cade exclaimed, his grey eyes wide with wonder.

Sylvie wasn't sure if her husband was startled by the measurements or the fact that Maggie had bent under two horny Warmblood stallions with a tape measure. The answer came rather quickly.

Cade roared with laughter, his belly jiggling up and down like Santa Claus in the middle of shouting 'Ho, ho, ho'.

The smell of beer and pussy wafted off of him in waves.

"You've gone to the strip club again, haven't you," she eschewed him, more miffed than outright angry. A leopard couldn't change its spots, as they say, and Cade O'Hara loved the ladies. Even half bald and sporting a paunch, his sparkling eyes and quick wit enamoured him to anything with an X chromosome. She had resigned herself to that far too many years ago to count.

Sylvie's father had said to her on her wedding day, *"Even good marriages are uphill battles. You don't have to go through with this. You can just walk away."*

Her father had been an expert judge of character.

"I thought you gals would still be partying," he shrugged helplessly.

"You bastard," Maggie spat, rounding on Sylvie's husband. *"What have those strippers got that I haven't? I'll tell you what they don't have... experience."*

Sylvie winced.

"That's enough, Maggie. You've had too much to drink," Cade ordered, trying to placate the disgruntled woman.

It was finally out in the open, Sylvie thought.

Sylvie broke away from her husband.

"Sylvie, my sweet dear girl," Cade stuttered. "Let me get you home. Maggie's drunk. She doesn't know what she's saying."

Sylvie looked deep into Cade's grey eyes and saw the truth in them. Despite his numerous affairs, she loved the man. He made her laugh. He held her close when the world came down upon her shoulders and she could do nothing but weep endlessly for her losses... and they were many... her parents, her two best hunters, the pony she had loved for thirty-six years, their daughter's tragic death when she was only five years-old, and then finally her breasts and uterus to cancer.

Her heart split in two.

A stabbing pain shot through her right arm and down her right side. Her face felt numb. She grabbed her chest with her left hand, her right arm feeling like lead, and felt herself toppling over, the world whizzing by above her head as she cascaded towards the floor.

"Sylvie," Cade cried out as Sylvie slipped to the floor. "Maggie, call 911."

"What's the matter," Maggie snorted. "Don't be silly, she's just faking it."

"You selfish callous woman," Sylvie heard Cade yell at Sylvie's once best friend before everything went dark.

And then Cade moaned, his eyes flickering open.

"Mags," he croaked.

"No, dummy, it's your wife," Sylvie rumbled.

Sylvie grabbed a pair of Maggie's silk underwear and straddled her husband the same way that Maggie had earlier.

"Sweetie," he said, recognizing his wife. "It's a miracle."

"Not really," she smirked.

Sylvie stuffed the lace panties down Cade's throat. She covered his mouth with both hands and waited. She had wanted to do that for a long time, dreamed about it even.

Cade tried to fight, his eyes widening in shock and disbelief, but to no avail.

Years of lies and endless affairs disappeared into the cosmos when the light went out of Cade's eyes. Still, Sylvie felt nothing. There were no more tears to shed over Cade O'Hara.

Sylvie heard the ladies muffled whispers outside of the door. The girls were returning to the scene of the crime.

Sylvie slammed Cade's mouth shut so they wouldn't see the red silk underwear stuffed down his throat, and then rolled over to the far side of the bed, slipping down to the floor to hide from view.

"It's settled then, we'll throw his body out the window and bury him in the manure pile until we can think of a better way to dispose of him," Zoe whispered conspiratorially as she staggered into the room.

"Okay, but what will we tell everyone again when they notice he's gone," Maggie asked, her sultry voice hoarse from all the brandy.

"We'll say that Cade told us he was leaving and there was nothing we could say to stop him," Zoe drawled, looking down at the body.

"Why was he leaving?"

"Oh, Maggie, he was having an on-line affair of course," Zoe said, wrapping an arm around her new best friend.

There was nothing like murder to bring two women closer together.

"Right, and he left me to be with her," Maggie giggled. "He did it once already. Did you know that?"

"He did not."

"He did," Maggie said triumphantly.

"Shhhh, you're talking too loud," Zoe whispered, putting a finger over her mouth.

"Shhhh," Maggie replied drunkenly back.

"Open the window and we'll toss him overboard," Zoe told her cohort.

"Just like on the Titanic," Maggie slurred.

"The Titanic hit an iceberg, Mags," Zoe scoffed.

"Whatever," Maggie replied flippantly.

Maggie fumbled with the window latch. It took some time, but she finally got it open and slid the window up as far as it would go.

Had Maggie looked a little more to her left, she would have seen Sylvie lying on the floor in utter amazement. This was all news to Sylvie. She had no idea about the internet affair. How many affairs had Cade had?

"'Kay, got it," Maggie said.

The two women each picked up an arm and dragged Cade's body to the window, grunting hard with the effort. With a soft bang and a thud, they propped the top half of his body out of the window and pushed. Cade's beer belly got hung up on the window frame, too wide to fit through the narrow opening.

"He's stuck," Maggie complained.

"Squish his tummy up," Zoe suggested.

They took a moment to catch their breath and then squished his sides together and pushed harder until finally his body fell to the ground below, shattering a tiny cedar shrub that fought for a toe hold in the hard packed earth.

"I didn't realize he was so heavy," Zoe gushed.

"Funny he never felt that heavy to me," Maggie mused, "but then he wasn't such a dead weight at the time."

"Well, you've got fifty pounds on me," Zoe quipped, "I mean look at you, you're an Amazon compared to me."

The women looked at each other and giggled.

Sylvie put her hand over her mouth, smuggling a laugh.

"Okay, let's go bury the body," Zoe said, heading for the door.

"What about his clothes," Maggie asked worriedly, starting to sober up. There was nothing like disposing of a dead man to bring one to one's senses.

"What about them," Zoe asked, confused.

"We can't say that he ran away into another woman's arms and leave his clothes behind," Maggie stated, indignant.

"Excellent point," Zoe murmured.

Sylvie swore under her breath. Now what?

"Wait, what about his truck," Zoe worried.

"Oh, that's registered in Sylvie's name," Maggie said, waving Zoe away. "Let's get going. We'll deal with his clothes after."

Zoe looked out the window at the crumbled body down below, legs splayed sideways, and one arm bent at an unnatural angle.

"How're we going to move him," Zoe wondered aloud.

"Oh, Heaven's, we'll just go get the manure cart," Maggie sniffed. "That's where he's going anyway... the manure pile."

"Mags, he was your lover and a human being after all," Zoe chastised her friend. "And he was okay in bed, not outstanding, but I've had worse."

"I suppose next you'll want a Scottish Highlands Band complete with pipes to send him off into the great beyond," Maggie declared, pushing Zoe towards the door.

"Oh, that would be nice," she beamed.

"Let's go," Maggie scolded her. "It will be light before you know it."

Sylvie crawled out from beside the bed after they'd gone, trying not to laugh. Zoe was outrageous and Maggie was... well... Maggie.

She didn't blame either woman for sleeping with her husband. He was a charming rascal.

Sylvie cautiously looked out the window at Cade's lifeless body. It was sad seeing him laying there like a puppet without a string. She felt a tinge of sorrow. She was grateful for that; after all, she had loved him once and knew that in his way, he loved her back.

Sylvie tip-toed out of Maggie's room and back down the stairs to her own room, carefully pulling back the covers and tucking herself into bed as best she could when she got there. The women would be back to clear out Cade's clothes before she knew it and she needed to look every part the invalid. She thought of packing his suitcase for them, but... only for a moment.

"You go get the poo cart," Maggie told Zoe.

"Why should I do it, you killed him," Zoe quipped.

"Because you're the last woman to sleep with him," Maggie reasoned. "That makes you an accessory."

"Oh, I've never been an accessory, darling," Zoe preened.

"Fine, I'll get the poo cart," Maggie declared, storming off to the barn.

Zoe glanced down at Cade. She shivered and looked after Maggie. She saw her roll back the barn door and disappear inside.

Night things buzzed all around her. They chirped and croaked and clicked. The noise made Zoe nervous.

What was taking Maggie so long?

Finally, Maggie returned with the manure cart. It squeaked annoyingly as she rolled it quickly across the yard.

"God, that noise will wake the dead," Zoe's voice warbled.

"Shhh. That's Sam's bedroom. Don't wake him up. Come on, hurry, help me load the body into this dreadful thing," Maggie said, bending over to lift Cade.

Zoe grabbed the dead man's other side.

"He really is fat, isn't he," Maggie mumbled.

Zoe grunted and heaved Cade's body up with all her strength. He tilted sideways and fell over. It took three tries, but she and Maggie finally slid the body bum side down into the manure cart.

"Help me push him," Maggie ordered her accomplice once again.

Zoe sighed, annoyed at being told what to do, but she was in over her head now. She gripped the wheelbarrow handle with both hands. Maggie lifted the other side. Together they pushed the cart across the yard.

They were three quarters of the way to the barn when the light went on in Sam's bedroom, followed by another light in the living room.

"It's Sam," Zoe squeaked.

"What should we do," Maggie barked, looking down at the man she had just murdered.

"Put him in a stall," Zoe suggested.

"Which one?"

"Which horse won't get upset over a dead man in a wheelbarrow sharing his stall?"

"Ah, gotcha," Zoe quipped.

They huffed and puffed and quickly pushed the wheelbarrow into the barn.

The front porch door squeaked open.

The ladies stood in the darkened barn watching Sam stroll across the yard, rifle in one hand.

"Oh my gosh, he will kill us," Zoe said sharply.

"No, he won't," Maggie growled. "Push!"

Zoe and Maggie stopped in front of Sylvie's stallion's stall. He eyed them quizzically.

Maggie popped the latch on Buddy's stall and signalled for Zoe to help her roll the dead man into it. The horse snuffled Cade's lifeless arm and looked at the two women in puzzlement.

"Sorry, Buddy," Maggie said, stroking the stallion's nose.

They leapt out of the stall, slipped the latch shut, and then ran to Zippo's stall. They were about to hide inside it when Sam turned on the barn's lights.

"What the devil are you gals doing out here," Sam growled seeing the two nightgown clad women standing in front of the Andalusian's stall door.

Zoe looked blankly at him.

Maggie raised her hands in frustration.

"Oh. Zoe's out for a midnight ramble again," Sam said, understanding dawning on his face. He propped the rifle against the wall.

"Yes, she is," Maggie agreed. She gently picked up Zoe's hands and stared pointedly into her eyes.

Zoe got the drift, although she had no idea what Sam was talking about.

"Zoe. Zoe, can you hear me," Maggie said, releasing Zoe's hands and grabbing her by the shoulders. She shook her gently.

"What," Zoe stammered, putting on one of her best performances.

Sam strode towards them.

"Come on, Zoe, let's get you back to the house," the worn cowboy hissed, pushing Maggie away, and wrapping an arm protectively around Zoe's shoulder. "I don't know how you found the key to the front door. I guess I must have forgotten to lock it before I went to bed."

The touch of Sam's callused hands on her skin made Zoe tremble. He was so much sexier than Cade.

Wait, she thought, *why was he locking the inside of the front door at night?*

"Jeepers, you're shaking," Sam said to Zoe, pulling her even closer.

Maggie rolled her eyes behind Sam's back, mouthing the words: 'go with it' to Zoe.

"Sam, what are you doing in my room," Zoe asked, feigning puzzlement.

"You were sleepwalking again," Sam answered.

Maggie gave Zoe a thumb's up sign.

"What do you mean 'again'," Zoe and Maggie asked together.

"Isn't that why you're out here," Sam said, picking up his rifle and handing it to Maggie.

"Yes, of course," Maggie agreed quickly, holding the rifle at arm's length.

Sam continued to gently lead Zoe out of the barn.

"Shut the door, will you, Maggie," he asked the raven-haired woman.

Maggie bristled. She hated being told what to do.

Zoe motioned for her to do what she was told. Maggie grimaced and shut the barn door behind them.

"What about Cade," Zoe mouthed to Maggie over the top of Sam's arm.

"Later," she waved to her friend.

"What's that, Miss Carroll," Sam snapped annoyed with the woman's dilly dallying.

"I was just saying how heavy this door is," Maggie quipped.

"All the better to keep cougars out," Sam drawled.

Maggie shrugged helplessly.

Zoe shook her head, trying to shut the woman up. Maggie's mouth pinched together into a thin line, her eyes glittering with an icy fire.

One of them would have to get back out to the barn to move Cade's body before BJ got up to let the horses out in the morning, and neither knew how they would do it.

Sylvie heard Sam escorting Zoe and Maggie back up to their bedrooms. She quickly scooted out of bed and lifted her window up. A cool breeze lifted her hair. She brushed the stray strands out of her face.

Sylvie slipped a small pen light into the pocket of a sweater and tugged the sweater over her head. She then donned a pair of beat up sneakers and threw one leg over the windowsill, climbing out into the night.

A groan escaped her as she raced across the yard, arms pumping. She was too old for these shenanigans. The wheelchair would be a necessity in the morning.

Hair and nightgown flying out behind her, she ran around to the rear of the barn, certain that Sam wouldn't be able to see her. She slid open the door and stepped into the blackness inside the barn.

The smell of horses, hay and manure greeted her.

There were muffled sounds coming from all the stalls. Most of the horses were sleeping.

Sylvie flicked on the pen light.

She paced up and down the barn, unable to locate the wheelbarrow with her dead husband in it.

"Where on earth could those damnable women have hidden him in such a short time," she growled.

She was about to give up when her horse nickered softly.

"I'm sorry, Buddy, I'm in a hurry," she crooned to the horse.

The horse shuffled its feet and nickered again.

"What's wrong, Bud," she asked the towering Hanoverian.

She shone her light across the giant bay's body. The light reflected off Cade's glazed over eyes.

Sylvie gasped in fright. At least it wasn't a cougar, she thought grimly.

Steeling herself, she opened the stall door and calmly pushed her stallion to one side. The horse obeyed her command and stood quietly against the wall.

Sylvie heaved and grunted, trying in vain to get the wheelbarrow with the body in it out of the stall. Finally, she could half lift and half drag it across the floor, but it took all her strength.

"I told you to eat more greens," she huffed, wiping the sweat from her face. Her husband was a beer and burger man, and it showed.

Sylvie stopped for a short breather.

She tossed a flake of hay into her stallion's stall and gave him a kiss on the nose. The Hanoverian settled down, happy that the dead man had been removed from his stall.

Sylvie braced herself and continued to half drag and half lift the manure cart until she had it at the back door. It took her almost twenty minutes to wheel Cade outside and partially across the rear paddock towards the manure pile. She stopped to rest several times and once to close the barn door.

The manure pile was now six feet high and about twenty feet across. Cleaning six to twelve stalls every day created a lot of tonnage.

Somewhere in the night, a coyote howled, and she thought she heard a cougar growl.

That would solve all her problems and Maggie's too. The cougar could chow down on Cade all it wanted. It was a mean thought, she knew, but she couldn't help herself.

"I'm sorry, dear," she whispered to Cade's inert form. "I should have divorced you years ago, but then our daughter died, I got cancer, and I had that damned stroke. Life kind of got in the way, didn't it?"

Sylvie push-dragged the body up beside the outhouse and leaned against the sage green wooded sides.

The lights went on in the barn.

Sylvie choked down a fearful cry and looked around, terrified. What should she do? Sam will call the sheriff and she'd spend the rest of her life in a jail cell.

"Not going to happen," she hissed.

She flung open the door to the outhouse and pushed the cart forward. It tipped onto its nose, sending Cade's body flying forward. He landed on the outhouse seat facing the wall.

Sylvie pushed the manure cart towards the riding ring and bolted back across the yard to the outhouse. She flung open the door, turned off her penlight, and softly closed the door behind her, trapping her inside the outhouse with her husband's body.

She looked out the peephole in the outhouse door.

Sam opened up the barn's back door, the light behind him illuminating his slim athletic form. His cowboy hat dipped and then straightened as he searched the outhouse and the pasture beyond for any signs of the cougar.

Sylvie heard the cougar's call. The growl set her nerves to tingling.

"Git, you hear me," Sam yelled. "There's nothing here for you."

Sylvie waited.

She saw Sam lift the rifle to his shoulder.

She thought he would fire off a shot, but then he lowered the gun.

Sylvie held her breath as he walked towards the outhouse. Damn, but she didn't want to go out like this, not hiding in terror in an outhouse with the man she had once loved resting atop an outhouse seat, dead to the world.

Sylvie squared her shoulders, stuck her chin in the air, and with a forced bravado, waited for Sam to open the door. Instead, Sam gathered up the manure cart and took it back to the barn without as much as a backward glance.

Sylvie let out a sigh of relief.

Sam slid the barn door closed. The lights went off in the barn.

Sylvie glanced at Cade.

"Even dead, you're still a pain in the ass," she chastised her husband.

With some effort, she rolled Cade over and propped him up on the old toilet seat. She noticed that there was a new issue of a Western Horseman magazine tucked inside a brass railed rack, and the hurricane lamp smelled like it had been lit recently. There was also a tiny silver pocket sized flask half full of whiskey.

Sylvie grinned and took a swig of Johnny Walker.

God bless Sam Montana, she thought as she slipped out of the outhouse, latched the door behind her, and then headed back to the house, stealthily walking through the night to avoid detection.

Tomorrow was another day. She'd figure out what to do with Cade then. She had at least ten hours to do so since Sam, the sheriff, and all the other ranchers would be off hunting the cougar.

The thought of having to ask the ladies for help made Sylvie blanch, but she figured she'd cross that bridge when she came to it.

Chapter Fifteen

There's no shame in fear. But understand this - the coward is ruled by fear, while the hero rides it like a wild stallion.
David Gemmell

Sam and BJ were up early. Their friends and neighbours would start arriving at around nine after they had fed and watered their own livestock.

The cougar had taken down a calf at the Diamond Bar ranch to the south of the Montana's spread during the night so a half dozen of the cowboys from there would join the hunt for the cougar.

Sam and BJ were surprised to find Zoe milling about in the barn when they opened the door. The petite woman was going from stall to stall, looking into each of them with a frown on her face and an overall puzzled expression. Sam prayed that she wouldn't start wandering at all hours of the day too. The night was a worry enough.

"Mrs Puddicombe, what're you doing up so early," BJ asked his riding instructor.

"Zoe, remember," she idly said, leaning over Sylvie's stallion's stall door.

"I know, it's hard for me to call you by your first name," the boy blushed.

Zoe turned around and fixed the boy with a brilliant smile, the stallion behind her playfully nibbling on a strand of her porcupine hair. Zoe wagged a finger at him and stepped away from the stall.

Sam sighed with relief. Zoe was simply up early this morning greeting all the horses.

"The next time we go into town, you must come with us, BJ," she grinned happily. "You can help me pick out a cowboy hat too. Maybe you'll find it easier to call me Zoe if I look the part of a cowboy grandma."

BJ and Sam laughed aloud.

"If you want to let your stallion and filly out, I'll take out their hay," BJ offered.

"Or give them a brush down," Sam suggested, "since they haven't had their grain yet."

"I've already spoiled all the horses this morning," Zoe crooned, giving the bay stallion a quick pat. "I think I'll go grab a cup of coffee at the house."

With a shake of his head, Sam wandered off to the feed room. There was no understanding the ways of a woman.

Zoe cast a curious glance Sam's way as she left the barn.

Sam returned from the feed room carrying four buckets.

The ranch horses nickered softly, waiting to be fed. As always, the grey filly banged a leg impatiently on her stall door. The donkey hee-hawed, and three of the four stallions whinnied shrilly.

As Sam walked by the door, he noticed Zoe catching Maggie by the arm and leading her back to the house. The two ladies whispered heatedly back and forth until they turned their backs towards him, and he couldn't tell if they were still talking or not.

Sam appreciated Zoe cutting Maggie off. He didn't feel like dealing with her snide remarks or complaints. He'd deal with her and the two O'Hara's tomorrow. Hunting down that cougar took precedence over everything.

"BJ, I want you to take your time doing your chores today," Sam called to his grandson. "The Doc said you have to take it easy for a few days."

"Okay, Grandpa," he said, his cheeks already flushed from manhandling a seventy-pound square bale of hay into the hay cart.

"And that includes what you're doing," Sam scolded him. "Break that bale into two. Actually, never mind that, leave it me and I'll take the hay out to the turnout paddocks."

"Are you sure? I can do it," the teen sulked.

"I got it," Sam replied. "You do the buckets and give Checkers and Bucky extra grain. Gus called this morning. He's going to join the hunt. He can ride Bucky."

"Did he give up looking for that smuggler," BJ asked, taking the feed buckets from his grandfather.

"Looks like it," Sam answered.

Sam picked up the hay wheelbarrow. Most farms kept one wheelbarrow for hay and another separate one for mucking out. He passed by the manure cart on the way out the door.

It was a beautiful morning. There were a few clouds scattered about the sky, mostly over the mountains. Dew glistened on the metal gates and the top of the split rail fencing, but it wasn't heavy enough to soak the earth.

Sam split the hay up into four, tossing three large flakes into each of Buddy's, Zippo's, Storm's, and Extravaganza's paddocks. He then wheeled the wheelbarrow back to the barn, stopping at the little green outhouse to pick up his pocket-sized whiskey flask.

Yesterday had been a tiring day. A quick nip to fight off the arthritis pain in his knees would have been helpful. There were several other men who would have appreciated it too by four o'clock.

Sam examined the outhouse. It wasn't functional anymore, just decorative. He had laughed when Emma instructed him to paint it green on the outside and a dark grey-blue inside. She had even had Sam strip and re-glaze the oak seat. It was quite a comfortable spot to runaway to when he'd had enough of the women.

Sam opened the door and darned near dropped as dead as the occupant inside. Cade O'Hara sat facing him on the closed toilet seat, his body propped up against the back wall, his sightless eyes staring at Sam. Sam's mouth fell open in dismay.

There was something red sticking out of Cade's mouth. Sam stepped in and reached for it. He pulled the bit of silky red fabric out of Cade's mouth, knowing that he should probably call the sheriff and let him do it, but Sam couldn't help himself. The red bit of fabric turned out to be lady's silk underpants.

"Grandpa, do you want me to turn the ranch horses out first or leave them in until everyone rides out this morning," BJ yelled at him from the doorway to the barn.

Startled, Sam stuffed the red underwear in his pocket, stepped back and slammed the outhouse door shut, forgetting all about the silver whiskey flask on the floor.

"Leave 'em in," he called back, his voice crackling like a broken radio.

All at once he heard a commotion coming from the house. A loud wail of grief ululated through the still of the morning.

Sam broke into a run, BJ hot on his heels.

"What's all this about," Sam demanded, racing into the kitchen.

He stopped short.

Jenny wailed and hugged her mother around the waist, her tear-streaked face cherry red. She hiccupped and wailed even louder.

Mary and Zoe sat at the table, their faces tear stained and distraught.

Maggie sipped on her coffee, totally nonplussed by the goings on.

"Cade's gone," Sam's granddaughter cried.

Sam scowled. *He was gone all right.*

"Cade told Maggie and Zoe that he was leaving last night," Emma explained.

"Really," Sam growled. "That's interesting."

Zoe looked up, startled at the timbre of Sam's voice.

"Some bimbo he met online," Maggie added flippantly.

Sam looked askance at her.

"He's done it before," Maggie stated, looking pointedly at Sam. "He always comes back."

"But he was my friend, and he didn't say 'Goodbye'," Jenny cried.

"She picked him up last night," Zoe interrupted.

"She did, did she," Sam sneered, tipping his cowboy hat back on his head.

"It's okay, sweetie, I'm sure he'll call us," Emma consoled her daughter.

"No, he won't. He's gone," Jenny sniffed, her little heart broken.

"What about Mrs O'Hara," BJ asked innocently.

"Oh my God, I haven't even gone to check on her," Emma erupted.

"I'll do it," Sam snapped. "All of you stay put!"

Emma's eyes went wide. Sam felt bad, but he wanted to talk to Sylvie alone.

"You want me to help you get her into her chair," BJ asked him.

"I got it covered, grandson," Sam growled.

Sam stormed off.

What a day already! His neighbours would arrive with their horses shortly, the ranger and the sheriff too, not to mention Gus Rodriguez, and there was a body of one of their boarders in the outhouse.

Sam knocked softly and then pushed the O'Hara's bedroom door open. Sylvie lay in bed, her salt and pepper auburn hair creating a halo around her head, her face as pale as her dead husband's, her hands trembling.

"Sylvie are you okay," he gasped, rushing to the bed.

202

"Morning, Sam," she croaked.

"If you don't mind my saying, you look awful," he said, looking down at the frail woman lying so still in the bed. "Wasn't something to do with a midnight excursion, was it?"

"What makes you ask that," Sylvie replied, eyeing him dubiously.

"These," Sam said, pulling the red underwear from his pocket.

"I don't do red," she grimaced, wincing in pain.

"You really are hurting this morning, aren't you," he sighed, placing the panties back in his pocket.

"Yeah," she whispered through gritted teeth. "Think I'll just stay put."

"Grandpa, it's a miracle," BJ shouted from behind Sam.

Sam spun around. BJ stood in the doorway; his eyes wide with surprise.

"Mom," BJ yelled, "Mrs O'Hara is talking."

"It's a miracle all right," he grumbled as his family, Mary, Zoe and Maggie all raced to crowd into the little room.

"Sylvie, is it true? Is it really you," Maggie crowed.

"Well, who else would it be, you ninny," Sylvie chortled. She tried to move, but pain tore through her back like a streak of electricity across a hydro line.

"Whoa there," Sam said, sitting down on the side of the bed and placing a gentle hand on her shoulder. "I thought you were going to pass out for a minute."

"Almost did," Sylvie gasped.

"BJ call the doctor," Emma commanded her son. "Tell him Mrs O'Hara's talking, but in a whole parcel full of pain."

"Yes, ma'am," BJ said, spinning like a top and racing back to the kitchen.

"I can't believe it," Maggie marvelled, her syrupy voice rising as she walked around the far side of the bed and sat down. She took hold of her friend's hands. "You're shaking."

"Getting old isn't…," Sylvie said.

"For the faint of heart," Sam finished for her.

"You said it, cowboy," Sylvie grimaced.

"That's so cool," Jenny chirruped, drying her tears. "I might not have Cade to play cards with anymore, but I got me another cowgirl gramma."

"Jenny!" Emma cried.

"That's enough, child," Mary said lightly, turning the girl by the shoulders and leading her out of the room. "Let's we girls get breakfast started."

"But I want to stay and talk to Sylvie," Jenny whined.

"How about we chat with her after the doctor sees her and tells us it's okay," Zoe said, joining Mary and Jenny.

"Oh, okay," Jenny agreed, taking hold of one each of Mary and Zoe's hands. She skipped forward. "We can make Sylvie a pancake and I'll bring it to her."

"Very well," Mary chortled.

"It really is a miracle, isn't it," the girl rejoiced.

"Yes, it is," Zoe replied with a backwards glance over her shoulder at the woman lying in bed, Sam on the one side of her, and Maggie on the other.

"I'm flabbergasted," Emma gulped, letting out the breath she hadn't realized she was holding.

"That's one word for it," Sam grinned. "Don't worry, you go on, we got this."

"Yes, we got this," Maggie repeated, waving Emma away.

Emma hung back for a moment, blushed, and then followed the others back into the kitchen.

"What's happened to Cade," Sylvie asked. "Where is he? Why isn't he here?"

Sam didn't know whether to believe the woman or not. She sounded earnest.

"Cade took off again, Sylvie," Maggie griped, squeezing her friend's hand.

"Where," Sylvie asked, pulling her hand out of Maggie's grasp.

No love lost there, Sam thought to himself. Not a big surprise, all things considered.

"The same as before," Maggie lied. "He met some hot young thing and skedaddled."

Sylvie closed her eyes and let out a long, heartbroken sigh.

Either she was a fantastic actor, or she didn't know that her husband was dead, Sam reasoned.

Tears fell from the prone woman's eyes.

"Ah, no," she wailed, her whole-body quaking with grief.

Sam started. He felt bad. There was no faking that kind of heartbreak. What had he been thinking?

He blushed guiltily.

"I'm so sorry, Sylvie," Maggie cried, the hard shell that was Maggie Carroll breaking. She crumpled, the tears flowing.

"I'll leave you two ladies alone for a bit," Sam croaked, standing up, pushing his personal feelings aside. The body in the outhouse wasn't going anywhere, and nobody except for Sam used the building anyway.

He handed Maggie a box of Kleenex from the bedside table before leaving.

Emma raced in. He put a steadying hand out to stop her and closed the bedroom door behind him, leaving the women to their privacy.

"Let them be," Sam told his daughter-in-law, "those two women got a lot of history to hash out." He didn't add that one of them was probably a murderer.

"You're right," Emma sighed, turning back towards the kitchen. "You knew about the affair?"

"Wasn't hard to spot," Sam acknowledged.

"The doctor will be here in an hour," BJ said, walking out of the kitchen with a crispy piece of bacon in his hand.

Several trucks rumbled into the yard and the front door burst open, a powerful Saint Bernard exuberantly pulling the ATF lieutenant into the house, spit balls flying everywhere.

"Sorry," he yelled, using all his weight to stop the dog's momentum.

The bright eyed Saint Bernard saw the bacon in BJ's hand and lunged at it. The bacon disappeared in one swift gulp.

"A Saint Bernard," Jenny squealed with delight. She threw herself atop the dog.

"Jenny, stop," her mother yelled, too late.

"Its okay, Bulldozer is friendly," Gus stuttered, hauling the dog away from BJ.

"What next," Sam mumbled.

"Hi, Bulldozer," Jenny gushed.

The dog drooled all over Jenny, BJ, and anything else in its way.

"I hope you don't mind," Gus said breathlessly. "Bulldozer is my cousin's dog. My cousin called me last night and asked me to take the dog for a few days. She had a family emergency."

"Your cousin never heard of a kennel," Sam muttered.

"I have her chain," Gus added. "I can tether Bulldozer outside the barn."

"I'll look after her while you're gone," Jenny said, throwing an arm protectively over the happy dog. She looked at her mother with eyes as big as the dog's and an arm-bending pout on her face.

Emma laughed.

"Go ahead," Emma agreed.

Sam tugged his hat down over his eyes, waiting for the next shoe to drop. He needed to tell Cole about the body, but things kept getting in the way.

"BJ help me saddle the horses," Sam mumbled, walking around the dog and heading for the peace and quiet of the barn, deciding to follow the path of least resistance and just give up for a while.

"I'll get your lunch ready," Emma called after her retreating father-in-law.

"He's not thrilled with me, is he," Gus asked sheepishly.

"He'll get over it," Emma grinned.

"The 'he' in question can hear you," Sam yelled as he let the porch door slam shut behind him.

BJ ran past Sam. He quickly saddled his buckskin gelding for Gus. Sam looked after saddling Checkers.

The sorrel gelding with the four white socks danced in anticipation. Sam smiled, the weight sloughing off his shoulders momentarily.

He double checked his Remington 30-06, checking the chambers and the action, before ramming it into the leather rifle carrying case tied to his saddle.

The dog dragged Gus across the yard, much to the amusement of the cowboys gathered there. Dee had already ridden in too. She sat atop her Quarter horse and laughed delightedly.

Cole pulled into the yard and unloaded his horse just in time to see Bulldozer knock the feet out from under the ATF lieutenant, sending him flying into the air. Gus landed with a thud.

Cole grinned from ear to ear.

"Guess we know why the dog's name is Bulldozer," Sam joked, offering Gus a hand up. Gus blushed, accepting Sam's help and getting to his feet.

"You ready to go shoot a pussy," Cole said, slapping the lieutenant on the back.

"Hardy-har-har," Gus rumbled.

The handsome ATF agent tied the dog to a ring in one of the support beams used to tie a horse up. The cable he used was thick and wrapped in plastic to avoid injury.

"I'll get her some water and throw a saddle pad down on the floor for her," BJ offered.

"Thanks, BJ," Gus replied. "Don't and I repeat 'don't' let your sister let her off her chain."

"Yes, sir," BJ grinned.

"Cole, you and I need to have a talk later," Sam drawled, pulling the sheriff aside.

"What about," Cole asked hopefully.

"Not what you're thinking," Sam replied, thinking he would tell him it was fine by him if he asked Emma out again. The way Sam looked at it, that was Emma's call and he had no say in the matter.

"It's something else, but it can wait until we get back tonight," Sam continued, slipping a foot in the stirrup and then throwing his leg over the saddle. "It ain't going nowhere."

Emma ran out to hand off two brown bags and a couple bottles of pop and water to Gus and Sam. Sam nodded a thank you and rode off to join the cowboys from the Diamond Bar Ranch.

"Thank you for looking after Bulldozer," Gus said to Emma. "I really am sorry for the inconvenience."

"Sure you are," Cole joked, watching the dog dig a hole the size of Texas in front of the barn door. Small and large rocks were flying in every direction.

"No problem," Emma said. "You guys just be careful out there."

"I will," Cole finished, wheeling his horse around. He then called back to Gus: "Come on, city slicker."

"City slicker," Gus barked. "Who are you calling a city slicker?"

Cole grinned and trotted off to join Sam, leaving Dee to help get Gus on the road.

Gus put a boot in the stirrup and effortlessly glided into the saddle. He picked up the reins and gave BJ's buckskin gelding a pat on the neck.

"You have ridden before, right," Dee asked the former marine.

"Yep, Cleve taught me in Afghanistan," Gus replied. "We spent three months in the mountains with the Kurds."

"You never told me that," Emma exclaimed.

"Oh, I thought I did."

"Nope."

"Guess I better spend some more time here then," Gus grinned.

Emma blushed.

"Take care of him, Dee," Emma told her friend.

"I don't think this guy needs any looking after," Dee laughed.

"Thank you for the vote of confidence, Ranger Dee," Gus quipped.

Emma watched Gus and Dee ride out together, the last two riders in a lengthy line up of cowboys that the ladies had dubbed 'the cougar posse'.

"You certainly have your hands full," Mary giggled.

Emma started. She hadn't heard Mary come up behind her.

"The hot ATF agent or the handsome sheriff," Mary joked. "That's a tough choice."

Emma wagged a finger at Mary.

"You mind your business, Ms Adams," Emma kidded the old woman, "or I'll sick Bulldozer on you."

"That's not going to happen," Mary crowed.

Emma slipped her arm under Mary's arm as they headed back to the house, the two of them laughing merrily.

"Which one would you choose," Emma whispered in the old cowgirl's ear.

"Oh, I am so not going there," the old barrel racer said.

Chapter Sixteen

*A man on a horse is spiritually as well as physically bigger
than a man on foot.*
John Steinbeck

Sylvie smiled at Emma and then the doctor.

Sylvie hadn't uttered an untruth her entire life until she started recovering from the stroke two years ago; now, the lies came so easily. She should have known better than to lift Cade the way she did.

"Well," the doctor told Sylvie and the three women and child gathered in the room, "you've got a heart like a lioness, but your back muscles are a mess from the years of inactivity. You've quite a serious sprain. Have you done any heavy lifting lately? That's the usual cause."

"Sylvie's been bedridden, Doc," Emma said.

"She spoke her first words in five years this morning," Maggie added, her lips returning to the thin-lined scowl that she habitually wore.

"I needed to pee," Sylvie whispered, the pain making her wince. "Cade wasn't here, so I forced myself to get out of bed. It took a lot out of me just walking to the bathroom and back."

"That's probably what did it then," the doctor mused. "Anyway, Emma, I'll leave you with a few Tylenol Two's and a small subscription. Muscle relaxants and a combination of heat and cold will work the best. Rest, as well. I'll recommend you to a physiotherapist, Mrs O'Hara. You need to build up your physical strength slowly."

"Whatever you say, doctor," Sylvie agreed.

"Thank you, Doc," Emma said from her post at Sylvie's bedside.

The doctor pulled out some pain killer samples from his bag and then wrote out a prescription for the rest of the Tylenol Two's. He closed this bag.

"That is one of the nicest doctor's calls I have ever had," the doctor said to Sylvie.

"It's a miracle, isn't it," Jenny piped up.

"The body is a miraculous thing, young lady," the doctor continued. "It can heal itself, but it takes time."

The doctor smiled, nodded at the ladies and made his way to the door.

"Jenny, go fetch a glass of water for Mrs O'Hara so she can wash down the painkillers the doctor gave us," Emma told her daughter.

"Okay, Mom," Jenny said before dashing off to the kitchen.

"I'm glad it's nothing more serious, Sylvie," Maggie mumbled.

"You mean like another stroke," Sylvie said pointedly, rubbing it in.

Sylvie blamed both Cade and Maggie in equal measures for the stroke that put her in the wheelchair. She had dealt with Cade. The jury was still out on whether she would ever forgive the sullen woman that stood at her bedside.

What ever happened to the two carefree girls of their youth?

Somehow life had taken a cruel turn. She and Maggie had gone from the best of friends to the bitterest of adversaries. The many betrayals were stamped into the lines in their faces. It wasn't a one-way street either.

The shear ferocity of the silence she had to endure after the stroke while her mind whizzed and buzzed along gave Sylvie ample time for self-review and to plot her revenge against the two people who had cut her to the bone without ever spilling a drop of blood.

She had suspected that Maggie and Cade were having an affair for years. Hearing it come out in the open though, that was another matter. Not to mention having to sit in her wheelchair and watch the love birds in action, unable to say or do anything about it.

"Don't worry," Emma said, leaning forward to give the bedridden woman a giant hug, "you'll be right as rain and up and about before you know it."

Sylvie smiled at the youthful woman whose blue eyes showed nothing but concern, a stray strand of curly red hair falling forward over her face as if with a mind of its own.

Jenny skipped in carrying a glass of water. She handed it to Sylvie with a smile as wide as Lake Superior. Jenny was the image of her mother. She reminded Sylvie of the daughter she had lost to leukemia so many years ago.

The Montana family were such honourable people, and Sylvie had lied to them and taken advantage of their kindness. Sam had suspected her all along, especially after she started sneaking into the stable at night to visit her stallion. She couldn't help herself; she had missed Buddy so much. Her horse was the only thing she had to live for. Cade and Maggie's decision to come here was a godsend.

A lump formed in Sylvie's chest.

What would her daughter think of her mother now if she had lived?

Shame bubbled like lava beneath the surface. It quickly erupted like Mount St Helen's.

Tears flowed as she realized the enormity of what she had done. Her fall from grace was staggering. A flood gate burst open, years of heartbreak and deceit rolling over her like a tidal wave.

Perhaps it was a preacher she needed and not a doctor.

Before she knew it, two women she barely knew, one young lady, and an age-old friend were by her side, comforting her and holding her hands.

In that moment, Sylvie knew what she had to do.

"I'd like to talk to Sam when he gets back," she croaked, gratefully accepting a Kleenex from Mary and dabbing at her eyes.

"Is there something I can help with," Emma asked.

Sylvie smiled sadly and shook her head. Her chest ached. She sobbed into the young woman's arms.

There was nothing Emma could do, nor Maggie or anyone else. This would be between Sylvie, Sam Montana, Sheriff Cole Trane, and God.

BJ played with the Saint Bernard for a while and then wandered off to finish his chores. He had mucked out all the stalls and was about to take out the afternoon feed to the horses, figuring he would water the herd at the same time, when he heard the dog's booming bark. A yip and a strangling sound followed it.

BJ stopped loading hay into the wheelbarrow and raced down the aisle.

"Bulldozer, hang on," he cried seeing the distressed dog down on the ground, the cable leash wrapped around her back legs and hanging in a hangman's noose around her neck.

BJ ran to the dog.

The dog gasped for breath; spit forming a puddle beneath her face as the noose around her neck tightened.

He tried to un-loop the cable from around her throat, but the knotted line snapped taut around her hind legs, making it worse.

"Hold on, girl," the teen cried.

The dog's tail thumped on the floor despite the pain that she was in.

BJ's heart throbbed in his chest. He had to help the dog.

"There's no other way," he mumbled, grabbing hold of the tie down clip and unhooking it from her collar.

He then gently un-wrapped the cable from around the dog's throat and back legs. The dog sat up, panting furiously. She licked his face. A trail of slime coated his hair and dripped down his cheeks.

"Oh, yuck," he cried, laughing as he pushed the dog's gigantic face away from his.

Jenny came bounding into the barn at the same time. The dog galloped to her and jumped up, sending Jenny flying.

"Bulldozer," BJ yelled, rushing over to his sister. He pulled the bouncing dog off her. "You okay, Jen?"

"Yeah, just gob-slobbered," Jenny grinned, her face and hair coated with dog spit.

"Me too," BJ laughed.

BJ helped his sister to her feet and then wiped the dog drool off his face with the corner of his t-shirt.

"You weren't supposed to let Bulldozer loose," Jenny chastised her brother as the dog ran back and forth across the yard, sniffing this and that, and having a splendid time.

"I know, but she was choking on her chain," BJ explained.

"Bulldozer, come here," Jenny called, chasing after the dog.

"Jenny don't run after her," BJ shouted in alarm. "She'll think it's a game and take off."

The Saint Bernard took one look at Jenny and made a beeline for the open gate to the main pasture.

"Oh, no," BJ yelled, racing to get to the gate before the dog did. "Nobody closed the gate."

Jenny raced after her brother.

The Saint Bernard scented freedom and bolted across the yard, through the gate, and across the grass pasture at a ground eating pace.

"Bulldozer," Jenny screamed, "come back."

"Bulldozer, come back," BJ echoed his sister.

Winded, the two kids stopped. They watched the dog jump into the creek, and run splashing through the water, heading straight towards the mountain.

"You are in so much trouble," Jenny said to her brother.

BJ blushed.

"Want me to tell Mom," Jenny offered. "Everyone will think I did it, anyway."

"No," BJ snapped. "I'm gonna saddle Penny and go after her."

"Mom will be pissed," Jenny hissed.

"What do you want me to do," BJ fumed. "I can't tell Gus I lost his dog and didn't go looking for it."

"I'm coming with you," Jenny said.

"No, you're not," he said heatedly.

"Yes, I am."

"No, Jenny," BJ finished, grabbing her by the arm. "It's my responsibility and someone needs to look after the horses. Just don't go in the paddock with Zoe's filly. She's got a nasty streak, and the same goes for Mrs Carroll's stallion. The others are okay."

"All right, but you're gonna owe me."

"Yeah, I know."

Brother and sister returned to the barn. Jenny fed and watered the horses while BJ saddled up his mother's mare.

"Be careful, bro," Jenny said to her brother as he grabbed an extra halter rope to lead the dog with once he found it.

"I will," he said, mounting his mother's rangy Quarter horse.

He trotted over to the gate beside the donkey and paint's paddock. The gate led out into a separate hay field. It wasn't visible from the house.

BJ prayed that the dog hadn't gone too far.

Jenny stood filling Mike and Patch's water trough, watching her brother ride off in search of the Saint Bernard.

She bit her lip.

There was no way that BJ could lead the gigantic dog back home without help. The dog would pull him off the horse if he tried to ride and lead it at the same time.

"What he needs is someone to take turns with him walking and leading the dog," Jenny said to the one eared donkey.

Mike gazed upon her with trusting eyes.

Jenny grinned. She dropped the water hose and ran back to the barn to turn the water off.

She then grabbed a rope halter and went into the riding ring to fetch her pony.

"Come on, Rosie," she said to the little red roan appaloosa. "We got us a Bulldozer to wrangle."

Jenny quickly saddled her pony and cantered off across the fields after her brother without a thought to the cougar at large or the rest of the horses who she had forgotten to finish watering.

The Saint Bernard frolicked in the creek, revelling in the scents and sounds of the grass fields and fresh flowing stream.

She scented rabbits and mice and the creepy crawly things beneath the earth. It filled her senses and made her drool with happiness.

Yes, she was happy. Her tail told the world just how happy she was.

The human children were marvellous. They smelled of bacon and eggs and the huge hairy things that liked to sniff her.

Bulldozer had never felt such freedom before and loved every minute, but some internal instinct was telling her she needed to return to the place of the humans and find a dark warm spot to curl up in.

She could feel it, the life that stirred inside her. It was like the tadpoles she chased in the stream, squirming and churning and moving around.

The urge to return to the ranch grew stronger.

She heard the human children calling, but they were a long way away now, and not in the direction that her instincts told her she needed to go.

The brown and white Saint Bernard galloped back across the pasture, listening to the call of nature and ignoring the rabbit that darted out of its den in the tall grasses.

She stopped to sniff the large dark brown creature. The giant hairy thing sniffed her in return. Time was running out though, and she moved along.

She ran back and forth amidst the buildings, but the machinery within those buildings stank. The liquid on the ground beneath the stacks of metal made her nostrils burn.

She paced back and forth, sniffing out place after place, until she found the squat building.

There was something meaty inside. The buzz of flies around it was incessant.

Unable to resist, the dog pawed and pawed at the door until the door swung open.

The dog known as Bulldozer sniffed the dead thing contained within the small hut. It smelled good but took up too much room in the den. While she hated to do it, the dead thing would have to go.

The dog dragged the dead thing over to the wonderful smelling heap of dung. Her instincts told her she may need the meat later.

Bulldozer prided herself on her digging abilities. She had proven time and time again how good she was. She didn't understand why the humans yelled at her for it. Here, though, in this soft damp wonderful smelling place, she could dig down deep.

The Saint Bernard examined her handiwork. The hole she had dug in record time was cavernous.

Bulldozer jogged back to the dead thing, grabbed a hold of the fabric behind its head and tugged it across the yard and into the mound of wonderful wetness.

Time was running out.

She had to hurry.

Bulldozer dragged the dead thing into the hole and quickly buried it, knowing that when she needed it, the dead thing would be there, fresh and meaty, seasoned by the moist wet earth.

Once done, she ran over to where the funny smelling grey beast and the brown and white taller beast were locked in their cage. She stuck her head through the fence, sniffed the grey beast, and then drank deeply of the water in the trough. It wasn't as good as the spring water, but it would do.

The Saint Bernard then jogged back to its den. She nosed the door, so it closed behind her as she entered and then curled up on the floor. It was now time to give birth.

Chapter Seventeen

A child's hope is that your father comes riding in on that white stallion and saves them.
Jake Roberts

Jenny trotted the red roan pony with the white blanket covered with blood-coloured spots on its rump along the creek bed.

She saw where the dog had rolled in the mud. Even for an eight-year-old, the tracks were easy to spot.

"BJ," she yelled, not able to see her brother anywhere.

"BJ, I've found Bulldozer's tracks," she hollered at the top of her voice.

The only answer was the wind rustling the tall grasses, the babble of the creek, and the frogs croaking in the marsh grass beside it.

"Bulldozer, here girl," she cried.

Jenny frowned. She shouldn't be out here, but she rode on anyway, unwilling to give up.

The dog appeared to be heading for the mountains, but suddenly the paw prints disappeared so she couldn't really tell. If Bulldozer got up into the high country, the cougar might get her. The thought of the giant Saint Bernard falling victim to the cougar made tears well up in her eyes.

"Bulldozer," she cried again. "BJ."

Jenny wiped away her tears. She was a Montana. Montana's didn't cry, they 'got it done', that's what her grandfather always told her.

"Let's go find Gus and Grandpa, Rosie," she snuffled, patting the roan mare's neck. "They'll know what to do."

Jenny wheeled the mare around and headed north, following the tracks that the sizeable group of rancher's horses had made in the hay fields. A six-foot-wide swath of a trail headed straight to the lower rock plateau below the mountain that overlooked the ranch.

Jenny followed the trail up to the rocky plateau, her pony picking its way carefully on the lower slope. The tall valley grasses and shrubs gave way to prickly bramble bushes and scrub pine. Dead and grey lichen, burnt lifeless under the summer sun, steadfastly clung to the granite face of the cliff wall that rose high above her at a ninety-degree angle.

A cool breeze brushed across her face, lifting her hair, but down in the narrow canyon ahead of her, Jenny knew it would be stifling hot.

Jenny looked down at the horse tracks in the dirt. The group of men had split up into twos and threes and went in all different directions. She wasn't sure which tracks were her Grandpa's horse, Checkers, or which were Bucky's.

"Grandpa," Jenny yelled, her voice echoing off the tiny canyon walls ahead of her. "Gus."

She sat on her pony and waited.

"We shouldn't go any further," the young girl told her pony. The pony snorted as if in agreement.

The pony's ears pricked forward.

Jenny thought she heard a dog barking.

The sound came from up the canyon she sat facing.

Jenny wasn't stupid, she knew that canyon. She had explored it with BJ many times. It ended about a quarter mile up and its sides were steep and rocky. In the spring, a river of water cascaded over the rocky bottom. There was a pretty water fall at the end where the snow melt came down from the tall mountain peak. There were also a lot of ledges that a cougar could use to pounce on an eight-year-old girl and her pony.

The sound came again. The pony swivelled its ears and snorted, facing the sound of the barking dog.

"Bulldozer," she screamed at the top of her lungs, her decision made. She had to rescue the dog. She kicked her pony forward.

Jenny rode cautiously into the canyon, letting her sure-footed pony zigzag around the taller of the boulders that dotted the wide canyon bed.

"Bulldozer, here puppy," she called, her voice hoarse.

Jenny's mouth was parched. She left in such a hurry she didn't think to bring water.

Sweat beaded her brow and hands. The heat inside the canyon was suffocating. Not a breath of wind blew down the trail. Her leather reins were wet, limp, and slippery.

Dust rose in slight mushroom clouds around the pony's hooves as it walked on, head bobbing up and down.

The trail grew narrower and narrower as the sides of the canyon closed in.

"Bulldozer," she called once more, reining in the pony. Her soprano voice echoed back at her.

"Here," barked a male voice.

Jenny shrieked.

She yanked on her pony's reins. The appaloosa reared. Jenny clung to her pony's neck. The mare wheeled around and snorted a warning.

"Help," called the strangled voice from beside the trail.

In the shade of a rock, Jenny saw a blistered and sunburned man with a shock of shoulder length black and white hair, bronzed skin, and deep wrinkles on his face. His lips were so parched they had split open in places. The man was wearing dusty and torn chino pants and a torn once white t-shirt. He had been out in the elements for two weeks and was clinging to life.

"Mister, are you okay," Jenny said, leaping from her pony and running to the downed man's side.

"Water," he croaked.

"I'm sorry, I forgot it," she cried.

The man grimaced, his brown eyes flickering open. He regarded the tow-headed red head looking down at him with concerned eyes, her hair a riotous mess about her slim shoulders.

"Are you that smuggler dude," Jenny asked him.

The man choked back a laugh. His brown eyes sparkled despite his dehydrated state.

"I am," he hissed, pain wracking his body. "Name's Tommy."

"Pleased to meet you, Tommy," Jenny said, extending a hand. "My name is Jenny Montana."

Tommy Cortez extended a shaky hand. Jenny shook it.

Jenny examined the helpless man. She knew he was too big to fit on her pony and too exhausted and hurt to help himself or to hurt her, plus he was as old as her grandfather, so he didn't scare her. She pursed her lips and thought hard about what to do.

Behind Jenny, her pony stood warily looking at the man, nostrils quivering. Rosie stood still, even though Jenny hadn't tied her to anything. The pony knew its job.

"I don't live far from here," Jenny said, "so I'll ride back and get help. My grandpa is up here somewhere too, and so is my big brother. With any luck, I'll find them. I got my cell phone, but it doesn't work in the mountains."

Tommy tried to smile, but only grimaced.

A loud growl echoed through the canyon.

Jenny looked up. Directly above her head, only twenty feet away, hunched the cougar that Dee Gallant and the men were hunting.

The cougar snarled at her. Jenny could see one front tooth was broken right down to the gum line.

Dried blood stains dotted its shoulder where both the paint and the Hanoverian stallions had bitten into its flesh.

The appaloosa pony screamed and reared, its fear and flight drive kicking the horse into high gear. It bolted up the canyon, heading for home.

"Rosie," Jenny shrieked after the departing horse.

The cougar prepared to pounce.

Jenny whirled around. She and the cougar locked eyes. Out of the corner of her eyes, she saw a large branch. She darted towards it and picked it up, brandishing it like a sword.

"Bad kitty," she yelled at the cougar. "You git! Go on, git out of here!"

Jenny puffed herself up, fighting to control the fear that welled inside her breast. Dee had told her that if she ever encountered a cougar, not to back down, and to make herself appear bigger than she was.

The cat grumbled, its tail flicking menacingly back and forth. It relaxed its stance and continued to stare down at the eight-year-old girl and the helpless old man.

Jenny reached into her jeans and pulled her cell phone out of her pocket. She remembered the story of the lady who scared away the cougar playing Metallica. She didn't know who Metallica was, so she didn't have any of their music saved on her phone, but she did have Amanda Lambert, Dwight Yoakam, Dolly Parton, and a few other western singers. Her mom loved Dolly Parton.

Jenny selected a song and hit play.

"Eat this," she hollered at the cat.

Dolly Parton's song, *Working Nine to Five*, blasted out of the little i-phone.

"Working nine to five, what a way to make a living," Jenny sang along with Dolly Parton.

The cougar snarled and took off for higher ground.

Jenny smiled; mission accomplished.

"My mom says that song's enough to scare any cowgirl half to death," Jenny advised the hurt smuggler. "Apparently it scares cougar's too."

Tommy Cortez closed his eyes. He had thought he'd seen it all, but he was wrong.

Emma was tidying up the kitchen when she saw her daughter's appaloosa bolt into the yard, stirrups and reins flapping. Sweat covered the red roan mare's neck and flanks. Foam flew everywhere.

Behind the pony raced Maggie's lean chestnut Trakehner stallion and Zoe's grey filly.

"Mary, Zoe, Maggie, I need you," she screamed, racing for the front door.

Where was BJ?

What had happened to Jenny?

And where was the damned dog, she thought, noticing that the Saint Bernard was off its tether and the barn door was lying open?

"What's going on," Mary called from the living room.

"What's all the commotion in the yard," Zoe said, walking down the stairs.

"Your stallion is loose, Maggie, and he's ripping around with Extravaganza and Rosie," Emma shouted.

"What is my stallion doing out," Maggie roared, running for the door.

"I don't want him near Extravaganza," Zoe wailed. "She's in heat."

"That's the least of my worries," Emma snapped. "My daughter's gone!"

Emma leapt off the porch, darted out of the way of the frantic filly trotting circles in the yard, step elevated, tail in the air, her eyes and nostrils wide and red rimmed.

"Whoa," Emma said, trying to calm the grey filly. "Easy, girl."

Emma stepped around the filly and snatched the appaloosa's pony's reins off the ground.

"I'll get some lead ropes," Zoe yelled, darting away from the gnarly stallion and across the yard to the barn.

"Whoa, Storm, easy boy," Maggie crooned to the uptight red stallion.

The stallion snorted and reared.

"Oh, stop showing off and settle down, you silly thing," Sylvie cooed, propping herself against the doorway.

"Sylvie, go back to bed," Emma ordered the old woman standing in a cotton nightgown in the front doorway.

"Not on your life," Sylvie quipped, and then said to her friend: "Maggie, don't go getting your head knocked off. That's my job."

"Whoa, whoa," Maggie continued to say to her stallion, casting a woeful glance Sylvie's way.

Zoe returned with two lead ropes, all she needed since her filly and the stallion still wore halters.

"I will be so mad if that bonkers stallion of yours bred my mare," Zoe seethed.

"You and me both," Maggie snapped.

"Will you two quit arguing," Emma growled. "My daughter is missing somewhere and there's a rogue cougar on the loose."

"Where's BJ," Sylvie asked, looking towards the barn.

"It's not like him to leave the horses gates open or let his sister ride off alone," Zoe noted.

"No, it's not," Emma cried, her panic level raising another notch.

"And the dog's gone too," Maggie noticed, snapping the lead rope's clasp onto the halter's clip.

"What dog," Sylvie asked.

"Oh, the handsome ATF agent dropped off a Saint Bernard before riding off into the sunset," Zoe chortled.

"Sunrise," Maggie corrected her accomplice.

"Whatever," Zoe said, waving her away.

The stallion snorted and danced around its owner. Maggie reached out a calming hand, and the stallion settled.

Zoe did the same with her Andalusian filly, catching up her prancing filly and murmuring soothing words in its ears.

Sylvie grimaced, one hand holding her sore back, and stepped down off the porch.

"What are you doing, go back to bed," Emma gasped, leading her daughter's exhausted pony towards Sylvie.

"Give me the pony, I'll look after her," Sylvie muttered. "You go find your son and daughter."

"Who am I going to ride," Emma cried fearfully. "Boomer's too old. If BJ's not here, then he must have ridden out on my mare."

"Take Buddy," Sylvie replied softly. "He's big, and he's strong. That cougar comes near you, he'll kill it."

"I don't know," Emma said, her hands shaking. "I've never ridden a horse like him before. He's so big."

"You'll be fine," Maggie said. "I know because I'm coming with you."

"Me too," Zoe agreed. "Zippo could use a little action and Extravaganza's too flighty."

Tears of gratitude formed in Emma's eyes.

"But Mrs O'Hara, I can't leave you alone," Emma moaned.

"I'm not alone, I've got Rosie," Sylvie joked.

"Come on, time's wasting," Maggie ordered the three women. "We've got horses to look after and others to saddle, plus an annoying child to save and a teenaged boy to yell at."

"Hah, you're still a pistol," Sylvie glowered at Maggie.

"And maybe you should put some clothes on since you are so determined to put yourself back in an ambulance," Maggie regaled Sylvie.

"Come on, Emma, let's get you a horse to ride," Sylvie grumbled, stumbling along. She led the sweat soaked pony towards the barn, her slippers kicking up dust bunnies in her wake.

"Thank you, Mrs O'Hara," Emma wept.

"Sylvie, please," Sylvie croaked.

Chapter Eighteen

When you are on a great horse, you have the
best seat you will ever have.
Sir Winston Churchill

Sam and Cole rode side-by-side down a wash, back-tracking across their trail. There was no sign of the cougar.

"Maybe the horses took a big enough bite out of him he slipped back into the mountains to die," Cole offered.

"Nah, I doubt it," Sam said. "There wasn't enough blood for that, but there was enough blood to tell us we're dealing with one dangerous cat."

The two men rode on in companionable silence, scanning the ground for tracks. There were signs of Mule deer and rabbits, plus the occasional coyote and black bear scat, but no pigeon-toed cougar's paw prints.

"There's something I need to talk to you about," Sam rumbled, reining in his horse, and staring up at the sky where a buzzard circled lazily above them.

"By the tone of your voice, it sounds serious," the sheriff drawled.

"It is."

Cole reined his gelding in beside Sam's horse and examined the turkey buzzard. Another bird joined it.

"Something dead has got their interest," Cole added.

"Yep, something is," Sam agreed.

The two men watched the buzzards' lazy circles.

"What's on your mind, Sam," Cole asked after a time.

"There's a dead man in my outhouse," Sam confessed.

"There's a dead man in your outhouse?"

"That's what I said," Sam grumbled.

"Who'd you shoot? It wasn't some feller after Emma was it," Cole joked, wondering if Sam was pulling his leg, or issuing Cole a warning to back off.

"Nope, not that," Sam mumbled. "It's Mr Cade O'Hara. I'm guessing either his wife or his mistress done him in. For that matter, it could have been some other woman's husband. I was so tired last night; a twister wouldn't have woken me up."

"Wait a minute. Wait a minute," Cole declared. "Isn't Mrs O'Hara in a wheelchair? She's darn near a vegetable, isn't she?"

"Not by half," Sam growled.

The sound of galloping horses filled the air. The earth beneath their feet shook.

Sam's horse squealed a greeting.

Emma, Maggie, Mary and Zoe galloped around the bend in the trail atop four snorting stallions, the gigantic bay Hanoverian, the flighty chestnut, the brown and white blued eyed paint, and the elevated white Andalusian. The horses were bold and beautiful, heads tucked in, eyes bright, mane and tails flowing out behind them.

"Holy Moses," Cole gasped. "I ain't never seen nothing like that before."

"Me neither. They are a sight," Sam whispered. "Don't mention the body in the outhouse."

"I hear you," Cole agreed.

"Dad," Emma shouted. "Jenny's missing."

"BJ too," Mary yelled.

The women reined their horses in beside the men's.

"What do you mean the kids are missing," Sam said, his eyes widening with fear.

"They ran after the dog," Mary added.

"It broke loose," Maggie said, her stallion pinning its ears at the two geldings. Maggie forced him to back up until he settled down.

"We haven't heard anything," Cole said.

"Or seen them," Sam agreed. "What the tarnation were those kids thinking?"

"They were worried about Bulldozer," Zoe smirked.

"They're kids, Sam," Mary scolded him. "Kids don't think; kids just do."

"We've got to find them," Emma gasped.

"We do," Sam nodded. "Cole, why don't you ride up the ridge and see if you can find any of the other men. Pass the word about the kids and the dog."

"Will do, Sam," Cole agreed.

"Thank you, Cole," Emma said, her voice cracking.

"Anything for you and the kids," Cole croaked, pulling his gelding up beside the bay stallion.

The stallion towered over Cole's stocky little Quarter horse.

"You look good up there," he grinned, and then spurred his horse forward and galloped up the trail, heading north up the mountain to the upper ridge line.

"Cole's right, that stud suits you," Sam told his daughter-in-law.

"Sylvie told me to ride Buddy," Emma said. "BJ rode out on my mare. Rosie came home, without Jenny."

"She who did not speak now speaks volumes," Mary quipped.

"She does more than that," Sam growled. "Let's go find those kids."

Sam rode towards the point where he saw one of the circling buzzards swooping down to the ground. Whether or not he wanted to, he had to check out what the birds had found first. With any luck, it was a dead cougar.

The four ladies trotted after the cowboy, leaving a cloud of dust in their wake.

Dee saw the buzzard circle in the sky and land somewhere in the dead canyon ahead of them. She pointed it out to Gus.

"What do you think it is," Gus asked the Ranger.

"Probably a dead rabbit or deer, but I want to check it out," she replied. "Those stallions took a piece out of that cougar. With any luck, those buzzards are eating cougar tenderloin."

The pair rode their horses up the dead-end canyon.

Dee glanced sideways at the handsome ATF agent. He caught her checking him out and grinned. Dee blushed.

Dee spurred her horse forward.

They rode around a bend in the rock wall and came upon Jenny chasing the buzzard off the unconscious man with a stick, swinging at the bird with all her might.

"You git out of here too," Jenny screamed. "Ain't no cougar or buzzard going to get us!"

"Cougar," Dee exclaimed.

"Buzzard," Gus nodded at the angry bird hopping along the rocky canyon floor, squawking indignantly.

"Ease up, Jenny, you've won," Dee said to the red faced, angry child.

"I ran out of Dolly Parton songs," Jenny said, blowing a stray piece of hair from her eyes while swinging the stick like a baseball bat back and forth in front of her.

"That's Tommy Cortez," Gus exclaimed, swinging out of the saddle.

"I know," Jenny scolded the agent. "He passed out about a half hour ago, right when these darned buzzards showed up. I was scared the cougar would come back too, so I couldn't leave him alone."

Dee and Gus exchanged a worried look.

"The cougar was here," she asked Jenny.

"Up there," Jenny said, pointing at the ledge above her head.

"What did you do," Gus asked.

"Me and Dolly took care of it," the girl crowed.

"We'll get the complete story later," Dee whispered.

"Okay," Gus agreed, striding over to the unconscious man.

"Can you help me get him up on my horse," Gus asked Dee.

"Definitely," the Ranger said, dismounting.

"What are you doing out here anyway," Dee asked Jenny.

"Oh, yeah," Jenny whined. "Sorry, Gus, but Bulldozer got loose and ran away. BJ's out looking for her too."

"Good Lord, BJ's out here too," Dee gasped.

"Let's get Cortez and Jenny back to the ranch and we'll ride back out and see if we can find BJ," Gus said, his hand on the smuggler's wrist, feeling for a pulse. "His pulse is weak."

"I didn't have any water, and the cougar scared Rosie," Jenny squeaked, her bravado evaporating. "Do you have any? I'm thirsty too."

"Grab my canteen from the saddle, Jen," Gus told her.

Jenny grabbed Gus' water canteen and took a few swigs of the hot brackish water. She then handed it to Gus.

Gus dribbled some water between Cortez's cracked lips. He moaned and coughed it out. The smuggler's eyes popped open.

"You're lucky to be alive, Cortez," Gus said.

"Don't I know it," he groaned. "If it wasn't for this little girl, I definitely wouldn't be."

"S'okay, Tommy, I got your back," Jenny beamed.

"Tommy," Dee and Gus said together.

"Yeah, Tommy was on his way to visit his grandkids when the plane crash landed," Jenny said. "He fell down and knocked his head. He doesn't know how long he was out for, but he couldn't move when he came too. Tommy didn't even realize he was in a dead-end canyon."

Dee, Gus, Jenny and Tommy Cortez looked up as the group of riders including Sam, Emma, Mary, Zoe and Maggie rounded the bend.

Emma galloped to her daughter, vaulted off her horse and threw her arms around her, tears running down her face.

"Momma, you're hurting me," Jenny gasped.

"Oh my God, I thought I'd lost you," Emma wailed, releasing her grip, but still hugging her child to her breast.

"You were right, Mom," Jenny grinned, her eyes bright, her face and hair coated with a layer of dust.

"About what," Emma asked her daughter.

"Cougars don't want to work nine to five either," Jenny said.

"Jenny and Dolly saved the day," Gus murmured.

Dee and Gus burst out laughing.

"What made you use music to scare away the cougar," Dee asked Jenny.

"You," Jenny cried and threw her arms around the Ranger.

Sam pushed back his cowboy hat and then dismounted. He looked down at the smuggler who had caused all the fuss.

"Let's get this fella some help," he growled, and took one of Tommy's arms while Gus took the other.

The two men hauled the former drug smuggler to his feet and loaded him onto Gus' horse. Sam used his cow rope to tie Tommy to the saddle.

Once Tommy was secure, Sam mounted back up.

Emma helped her daughter onto the back of the big bay stallion and then led the stallion over to a boulder so she could get back on him.

"I can't believe I'm gonna get to ride the Midnight Special," Jenny babbled.

"You've got something special waiting for you at home too," Emma told her daughter.

"What," Jenny asked excitedly.

"No riding privileges for two weeks and extra chores for a month."

"But, Mom, I saved Tommy," the girl wailed. "And we haven't found Bulldozer yet."

"The dog will find her way back to the ranch," Gus responded.

Dee was surprised the ladies weren't saying anything until she noticed Zoe and Maggie were sizing up the smuggler.

"Come on, Gus, you can ride with me," Sam said, offering the agent his hand.

"That's okay, I'll ride behind Dee," Gus replied, "that is if she doesn't mind?"

Dee grinned and moved her left foot out of the stirrup. Gus put his foot in the stirrup and swung up behind her.

Dee glanced at Emma. Emma shot her a thumbs-up. Once again, Dee blushed, her face turning the color of a summer sunset.

"Hmmm, you're not that bad looking," Zoe whispered to Tommy.

The smuggler chuckled despite being barely able to maintain consciousness while tied to the horse.

"Zoe, he's a bandit," Mary gasped.

"I like a bit of bad boy now and then," she quipped.

"Just make sure you leave enough to go around," Maggie warned her.

The three old women started cackling as they walked their horses back to the ranch beside the bandit, much to everyone but Sam's amusement.

Chapter Nineteen

Dead horses can't kick.
Bulgarian Proverb

The cougar limped across the pasture. It sniffed the air. Its belly gnawed with hunger. Pain rippled through its shoulders from the deep wounds the stallions had inflicted upon it.

It didn't want to return to the place of man, but it scented food. It needed an easy kill. Survival was everything.

It followed along in the tracks of the man child on the horse. The sour stink of fear came off the animal the man child rode. The horse knew it was being stalked.

The man child rode into the ranch yard, between the three pens, the one that previously held the one eared grey beast and the stallion that had hurt the cougar. The large grey horse while fearful of the cat was too young to take on. The cougar knew by instinct that it couldn't stand another blow from a horse's hooves or bites like the stallions had given it, so it left the little roan pony, old donkey, and white muzzled gelding alone.

The man child, though. He was weak and small, not much bigger than the cougar.

The cougar waited in the tall grass; silent, hidden, patient. Soon... soon, it would eat.

BJ led his mother's mare, Penny, into the barn and unsaddled her. He gave her a quick rub down and led her back outside and turned her loose in the paddock with his grandfather's retired cutting horse, the donkey, and Jenny's pony.

He breathed a sigh of relief. Jenny was home. At least that was one thing he didn't have to worry about.

He watched the Quarter horse mare lay down in the dirt and roll.

It disappointed him. He hadn't found the Saint Bernard. His heart sank at having to tell Gus that he had let him down.

BJ heard a deep guttural growl.

The horses whinnied a warning. The gelding and pony charged around the ring, blowing snot out their noses, their eyes wild. The grey filly reared inside her pen. Mike, the donkey, brayed a warning and stood his ground waiting for someone to deal with the problem.

BJ spun around.

The cougar sprang across the ground at lightning speed, barrelling towards him. BJ raised his arms in defence. It was too late to run.

A streak of white and brown caught the cougar in its teeth in mid air. The Saint Bernard slammed into the cat. The cat and dog tumbled over and over in the dirt.

BJ screamed and fell to the ground.

The dog staggered to its feet, its great mouth dripping with saliva. The cat struggled to get up, but the dog was upon it, gripping its neck between its humongous jaws and shaking the cat so hard that its neck snapped in two. In mere seconds, the battle was over.

"Bulldozer," BJ cried.

The dog jumped on top of the boy, sending him flying onto his back laughing. It licked his face, leaving great gobs of drool everywhere.

The cougar gasped out a last breath and went limp.

Sylvie staggered through the back door of the barn, cradling Sam's shotgun under her arm. She wore a jean jacket over her nightgown and had replaced her fuzzy slippers with riding boots.

"Well, if that ain't a sight for sore eyes," she said, looking at the boy on the ground, the Saint Bernard on top of him, and the dead cougar a mere four feet away from them both.

"Bulldozer just saved my life," BJ said, wrapping his arms around the giant dog.

The dog barked.

The horses quieted in their respective paddocks, sensing that the threat had passed.

"Well, if that doesn't beat all," she quipped, pointing the shotgun at the cougar and kicking it to make sure it was dead.

The dog's ears pricked up. It leapt off BJ and used its nose to pop open the outhouse door.

"Oh, no," Sylvie yelled. "Get away from there."

She limped forward. BJ stood up and followed her.

"Well, I'll be tarred and feathered," the old horsewoman crooned, looking down at the Saint Bernard and her ten puppies.

BJ poked his head over Sylvie's shoulder.

"We've got puppies," he bellowed.

"Wait until your sister sees those," Sylvie chuckled.

"My sister," BJ asked, puzzled. "Isn't she here?"

"No, your mother and the gals have gone out looking for her. Her pony came back without her," Sylvie replied, one arm hugging the boy.

"Oh, no," BJ wailed.

"She rode out after you and this little lady," Sylvie said, nodding towards the Saint Bernard.

BJ paled.

"If anything happens to Jenny, I'll never forgive myself. It's all my fault," BJ moaned.

"No, it isn't," Sylvie said, trying to calm the boy. "Life happens. One day you'll grow up to understand that."

"I've got to saddle Penny back up," BJ yelled, pulling away from Sylvie.

"Over my dead body," Sylvie scolded him. "Your mother and the ladies are on it. There are also enough men in the mountains that one of them is bound to find her and bring her home. Right now, you're going to help me drag that darned cat out to the front of the barn, so it doesn't spook the horses or disturb momma and her babies. After that, you and I will sit on the porch with a glass of iced tea and wait for everyone to get back."

"Yes, ma'am," BJ sulked, knowing better than to argue.

Sylvie glanced sideways at the proud momma standing protectively over her litter.

"What on earth did you do with him," she mumbled, closing the outhouse door on the Saint Bernard and her puppies.

Chapter Twenty

From the desert I come to thee, on a stallion shod with fire; And the winds are left behind, In the speed of my desire.
Bayard Taylor

Sylvie sat on the porch with BJ waiting for the cougar posse or Emma and the ladies to return with Jenny. She sat in Sam's favourite rocking chair, rocking gently back and forth, the shotgun propped on the little log table beside her. She snuggled down into Cade's old faded jean jacket and tapped her feet as she rocked. A half full glass of iced tea rested on the table beside her.

BJ had gone out to the barn to check on the horses and the new litter of Saint Bernard puppies when Sam galloped into the yard. Behind Sam trotted Cole on his Quarter horse and Emma on Sylvie's stallion, Jenny's legs slung wide behind her mother's, the horse much too big for an eight-year-old girl's stubby legs. Sylvie could have sworn that her stallion was smiling.

Gus rode behind Dee on Dee's rangy Quarter horse. They led BJ's buckskin gelding; the Mexican drug lord tied to Bucky's saddle. Zoe and Maggie rode beside Tommy Cortez, chatting endlessly to the poor fellow.

Mary pulled up the rear on her paint stallion, a grim smile on her face. Sylvie knew what Mary was thinking. If she had been in that posse, she would have stayed away from Maggie and Zoe too.

"Well, don't you look all frontier," Sam joked.

"That's me, Annie Oakley reincarnated," Sylvie grinned.

Sam grinned back.

"I got something for you over by the barn," Sylvie smirked.

"It ain't something dead is it," Sam asked.

"It is, but not what you're thinking," she said, her grin getting bigger.

Sam cantered to the barn and reined up short. His gelding snorted and pranced away from the dead thing lying on the ground.

Sam whirled his horse and cantered back to the house.

"You kill that cougar," he drawled.

"Nope," Sylvie chortled.

"BJ?"

"Nope," she said again.

The rest of the group arrived.

"What's going on," Cole asked, reining his horse up in front of the house.

"The Bulldozer did it," Sylvie crooned, keeping her eyes on Sam.

"Bulldozer's back," Jenny cried happily, sliding down off the horse.

"She sure is," Sylvie winked at Jenny, "and she brought us a present."

"What? Where is she?" Jenny danced up the porch and sat down in Sylvie's lap.

"Jenny, get off Sylvie. She's supposed to be resting," Emma scolded her daughter.

"That's okay, I borrowed some of your father-in-law's pain tonic and I don't hurt so much no more," Sylvie replied, hugging the red-haired girl. "Bulldozer left us each a present in the outhouse."

"Whoa, wait just a minute," Sam growled angrily.

"Its okay, Sam," Sylvie said, staring him down.

Jenny took off at a run. She skidded to a stop by the dead cougar, looked at it, smiled, and then disappeared into the barn.

"What's in the outhouse," Cole asked casually, eying Sam as he did so.

Sylvie laughed. She knew exactly what Sam was expecting, and it wasn't there. Sylvie had no idea what happened to Cade. She and Sam would have a chat about it later.

"Puppies," Sylvie laughed. "Ten not-so-tiny bundles of joy."

Sam rounded on Gus.

"You brought us a pregnant dog," Sam hollered at the ATF agent.

"I didn't know," Gus replied, equally angry. He slipped off the horse. "My cousin runs a dog rescue. Bulldozer only just came in. That's why she asked me to take her for a few days. She didn't want to leave a new dog with her pack when she went away."

"Sam Montana, you listen to me," Sylvie said, pushing herself painfully out of the chair. She picked up the shotgun and tucked it under her arm.

"That Saint Bernard saved your son's life and you better thank the Lord Jesus that Mr Hottie brought her here to stay."

Sam glared at the irate woman dressed in a nightgown, over sized jean jacket, and brandishing his shotgun.

"If you know what's good for you," Sylvie finished.

"I'd listen to her if I were you," Mary said, pulling up on her paint. "She's got a gun."

Mary leaned over and high-fived Sylvie.

"Great, puppies," Cole blurted out, trying to relieve the tension. "And they're in the outhouse?"

"Yep, the body's gone," Sylvie quipped.

Cole paled.

"What body," Emma gasped.

"So that's where it went," Zoe blurted out innocently. "We'd left him in Buddy's stall and when we went back, he was gone."

"Wait! What," Sam gasped.

"It's my fault," Maggie confessed. "I caught Cade cheating on me and Sylvie with Zoe."

"And she blew the proverbial gasket," Zoe added crisply.

"You know that there are two law enforcement officers present," Cole advised them.

Emma looked both confused and aghast.

"I confess, Sheriff, I strangled Cade O'Hara," Maggie drawled. She held out her hands for the sheriff to handcuff but didn't bother getting off her horse. "Take me away."

"No, you didn't, you ninny," Sylvie replied, using the shotgun as a pointer stick until Sam reached out and took it away from her. "I sneaked up into your room while you and Zoe were tying one on and stuffed a pair of your panties down his throat and watched him choke to death."

"And you think I'm dangerous," Tommy nudged Gus as Gus untied him.

"But we tossed him out the window and wheeled him out into the barn," Zoe wailed. "What happened from there?"

"How do you think I hurt my back," Sylvie griped, sitting back down with a thud. "Owww."

"You wheeled him out of the barn and deposited him in the outhouse," Maggie exclaimed. "And I didn't kill him, you did. Oh, that makes me feel better."

"That about covers it," Sylvie added.

"And I saw him there right before we rode out this morning," Sam agreed.

"So where is he then," Cole asked, looking from the ladies to Sam to Emma and back again.

"Don't ask me, I was in bed," Sylvie growled. "I can barely hoist up that shotgun and this glass of iced tea and Johnny Walker... or is it Jack Daniels? I'm not sure, but my back feels a whole lot better."

"And there are just puppies in the outhouse now," Sam asked her pointedly.

"And one cougar killing bitch," Sylvie nodded.

Mary chuckled. Zoe, Maggie and Tommy Cortez followed suit.

Cole looked at Gus, hoping for help.

"No body, no crime," Gus shrugged.

"He's right. Without a body, your confession's no good, either of you," Cole said, nodding at first Sylvie and then Maggie.

"You find my husband's body, Sheriff, and I will confess before God and anyone else who needs to hear it," Sylvie stated.

"We have some tired horses to look after and I need to get word to the ranchers that the cougar's been dealt with," Sam sighed wearily.

"While you're at it, honey, maybe you can ride over to the liquor store and replenish our arthritis medication," Sylvie grinned at the handsome white-haired cowboy.

Jenny raced across the yard with a puppy held tightly in her arms. Bulldozer towed BJ along after her.

"Mom, look, this one looks just like her mother," Jenny wailed. "Can we keep her?"

"And Bulldozer too," BJ asked breathlessly. "She saved my life."

"You need to stop making a habit of that, boy," Sam chuckled. "You're old enough to save your own skin."

"Yes, sir," BJ grinned.

"Give that dog leash to Gus and git that fella off your horse and climb aboard," Sam nodded towards the buckskin. "We gotta ride out and bring everyone in."

"Yes, sir," BJ chirped, "but who is gonna look after the Dozer?"

"I got that covered, kiddo," Gus said, taking Bulldozer's leash from BJ's hand.

Chapter Twenty-One

A horse is the projection of peoples' dreams about themselves--strong, powerful, beautiful--and it has the capability of giving us escape from our mundane existence.
Pam Brown

Summer gave way to autumn and autumn to winter. The manure pile out back of the barn grew higher and higher. Eventually Sam had to call a compost company to come and remove it.

Everyone at *The Silver Spurs Home for Aging Cowgirls* looked forward to the spring and the birth of Extravaganza's and Desert Storm's foal. A naming contest had already begun. Maggie and Zoe had finally loosened up and were happily awaiting the foal too.

Cole and Emma went to the honky-tonk most Saturday nights, and Cole was a regular for Sunday dinner.

Dee and Gus didn't quite gallop off into the sunset, but they did spend a lot of time together when Dee wasn't chasing poachers and Gus wasn't chasing smugglers, watching the sun go down and snuggling by the fire.

254

Tommy Cortez went to jail, but discovered that he was allowed conjugal visits and his two new lady friends were crazy. He didn't mind. He was still wild at heart too. Now, all he had to do was convince one of them to marry him. Unfortunately for Tommy, the ladies weren't born yesterday.

Jenny Montana was thrilled. Her dreams had come true. She had four cowgirl grandmas.

Bulldozer and Dozer Junior took up most of the space in front of the woodstove while the ladies played poker, all of them sporting brand new black cowboy hats. Sam steadfastly refused to take part.

Cade O'Hara was never found.

The End… okay, maybe not quite.

I hoped you enjoyed *The Silver Spurs Home for Aging Cowgirls*. The second book in the series is a rollicking kidnapping caper gone wrong, *Bandits, Broads & Dirty Dawgs*.

Please don't forget to leave a review. It will make this old cowgirl and her family very happy.

If you like **black comedy cozy mysteries with wayward pigs, a Jersey cow, and a whack of courageous dogs**, check out *Gumboots, Gumshoes & Murder*. It is a laugh out loud murder mystery series for those who enjoy Miss Marple, Murder She Wrote, or Glock Grannies.

Other Books by Laura Hesse

<u>The Holiday Series (family adventure)</u>:
One Frosty Christmas, The Great Pumpkin Ride, A Filly Called Easter, Independence and Valentino

<u>The Gumboot & Gumshoe Series (Cozy Mystery)</u>:
Book One: *Gumboots, Gumshoes & Murder*
Book Two: *The Dastardly Mr. Deeds*
Book Three: *Murder Most Fowl*
Book Four: *Gertrude & The Sorcerer's Gold*
Book Five: *Chasing Santa*

<u>The Silver Spurs Series (Cozy Western Comedy)</u>:
Book One: *The Silver Spurs Home for Aging Cowgirls*
Book Two: *Bandits, Broads, & Dirty Dawgs*
Book Three: *Who Killed Cade*
Book Four: *The Homecoming (2022 by fan request)*

<u>Paranormal Thriller</u>:
The Thin Line of Reason
Defying Hope

If you want to find out more about Laura Hesse or hear about her upcoming releases, then visit:
www.RunningLProductions.com

About the Author

Laura grew up a back stage brat in Music Hall Theatre and credits her mother with her love of song and theatre. She loves to sing at local jams when she can.

While all of Laura's horses have passed over the rainbow bridge, but they will forever live on in the pages of her books.

Made in the USA
Monee, IL
22 May 2022

96895215R00144